for Shirley

STANDING IN FOR LANA

HOLLYWOOD TALES

RICHARD FRATTALI

HAMMONASSET HOUSE BOOKS

Hammonasset House Books

64 Edgecomb Street
Mystic, Connecticut 06355
http://www.hammonassethouse.com

Library of Congress Cataloging in Publication Data

I. Frattali, Richard W. , 1935
II. Title
PR2301.F87 810.01
ISBN 978-0-9801894- 9-0
Manufactured in the United States

1. Hollywood–Social Life and Customs–Fiction
2. Fiction–Short Stories 3. Fiction–Literary
4. Fiction–General
I. Title

Cover photo, "Casting Couch," copyright © 2010 LAJ

CONTENTS

SHARKS

It's very awkward not being able to tell people where you work. When anyone asks me I make up something, but, as my grandmother used to say, a liar has to have a good memory, and I've had a couple of embarrassing moments when I've answered that question for one person in the presence of another to whom I'd previously lied. People out here are always asking you if you're working, and if you say yes they ask you what you're doing. It's one thing or should I say one of the many things that I hate about Hollywood.

Actually it's my choice not be truthful about my job. I've got a reason. I'm ashamed of it. I took the job at a time when I was desperate for money. I know a lot of people are, but I'm talking real desperation. First of all my rent was due, ten days overdue to be exact. My landlord, whose last name is Schmuck, so help me God I'm telling the truth, is not a nice person, and when money's involved he gets worse, like he becomes a son of a bitch. He hates actors which is kind of inconvenient in a town where every third person calls him or herself one, as I do. That isn't what I'm ashamed to tell people. When I work as an actor I brag about it. Most actors do.

Anyway, besides the rent being overdue I was behind two payments on each of my three credit cards, and they were charged up to the limit, so I couldn't borrow from one to pay on the others which I had been doing until, as my grandmother used to say, the chickens came home to roost. In addition to the credit card mess I was in, the brakes on my car were shot, and my dentist was telling me I had to have a root canal or risk major infection. I guess that's enough to make my point about being desperate.

I heard about the job, the one I do now that I'm ashamed of, from my friend Trini. Trini is a transsexual or I guess you'd say a semi-transsexual, since she's had her breasts enlarged but not the other part done. She claims she can't afford it but I suspect, and I have no way to prove it, that she just isn't ready the make that strong a commitment. I met her a couple of years ago when we were waiting on tables in a ribs place in Culver City, and I assumed she was, for want of a better phrase, a natural woman. She was small and cute with pretty dark curly hair and smooth skin. One night after work we went out for a few beers and got a little loaded. It was then that she told me about having a penis. I've lived in this town for a while now, and I've been around the block a few times if you know what I mean, but I almost shit when I heard that. I wasn't sexually attracted to her, thank God, but it still required a lot of adjustment on my part in terms of the way I related to her. For example I'm a person who likes to touch people. I put my arm around them and hug them and kiss them on the cheek a lot. Most people in show business do that. I'm not one of those guys who wants to have sex with every woman he meets, but even if you don't want to have sex with them you touch women differently from the way you touch men. After Trini told me she had a dick I didn't know how to touch her. If I caressed her the way I might caress a woman I'd picture it there between her legs, and it disconcerted me. On the other hand if I threw my arm around her shoulder or shook hands with her the way I might with a male if felt strange. I just stopped touching her altogether. If she noticed it she never said anything.

Trini had a boyfriend named Cesar who was a busboy at a fish restaurant out on the Pacific Coast Highway. Cesar would pick her up after work sometimes, and if you didn't know about Trini's package you'd think they were just another cute Latino couple. The ribs place burned down, on Christmas Eve would you believe, and I lost track of Trini for a couple of years. Then one day coming out of Samuel French's on Sunset Boulevard I ran into her. I had gone there to get a copy of The Zoo Story. My tuition was paid for three more weeks in the scene study class I was taking, and I wanted to do a scene from the play before my time was up, so to speak. I've already mentioned how desperate I was for money at the time, and I couldn't see how I was going to come up with any more tuition. I was unlocking my car when I heard someone say, "Jesus Christ, I thought you died." It was Trini.

Without thinking about the stuff I mentioned about touching I threw my arms around her and gave her a big hug. She was looking great, beautifully dressed and sporting a stylish haircut. We went for coffee. She was working as a receptionist in a modeling agency and living with a Persian guy who, she said, treated her like a princess. She said she'd had it with Latin men all of whom looked down on women except for their mothers and the Virgin Mary. She told me Cesar's family had forced him to marry his cousin from Managua and that they had a baby with another one on the way. She said he called her, but she didn't mess around with married men, because there was no future in it.

"There never was, and there never will be," she said, pushing away the empty dish her tapioca had come in. She asked how things were going with me. I told her the truth. I know there's a school of thought that says you should accentuate the positive and all that, but Trini isn't the sort of person you bullshit, and besides, I couldn't think of one positive thing to say.

"All I'm hearing is a money problem," she said when I finished.

"I'm glad you think it's nothing."

"I don't think it's nothing, but of all the

10

problems you can have it's the easiest one to solve."

"Right."

"If you told me you were sick or that you loved someone who didn't love you back I'd just have to sit here and listen, but I can help you with this one."

I was all ears.

"Manny, my boyfriend, runs a business, and he's always looking for good people. Manny isn't his real name, but Persian names put people off ever since nine eleven. Manny was as shook up as everyone else, but he can't wear a sign saying that, so he uses Manny and people think he's Italian or Greek. Anyway, he runs this telephone service, Talk To Me, where people call in to get their rocks off over the phone. They pay by the minute, and if you make a good connection they'll talk for hours. A lot of the callers are regulars some from as far away as Alaska. Jesus, can you believe some people? Anyway, you'd be perfect."

"Doing what?"

"Taking calls."

"I wouldn't know what to talk about."

"They train you. Besides, you're a natural with two good qualifications."

"What?"

"You're an actor, and you're broke."

"I'm not sure I could handle it. There's something about it that's awfully exploitative."

"There's something about you that's awfully

naïve, and it's time you realized it if you're going to survive in a sewer like Hollywood."

"What do you mean?"

"All markets are exploitative. That's the point of a market. Jesus, Forest Gump, where have you been all your life?"

I didn't say anything.

"Suit yourself. It pays twenty-five bucks an hour plus commissions, and you can work out of your home, any shift."

"Give me Manny's number."

When I called later that day Manny said Trini told him about me. He gave me an appointment for an interview the next day. "You've got the voice for it," he said.

I hate to admit it, but his saying that really puffed me up. I've had a lot of rejection in the course of my career, and for quite a while now I've been living with the fear that I made a terrible mistake in setting out to make a living as an actor. To be told I'm right for something, even by a pimp like Manny, was very refreshing. My grandmother used to say that if you want something badly enough you'll get. Most of what she said I've found to be true, but I'm not so sure about that one. I mean this town is full of insurance clerks and gas station attendants who wanted to be actors more than anything, and they didn't make it. I wish my grandmother was still alive, so I could talk this over with her. I'm sure she'd have some explanation or maybe she'd add something to it, and I'd learn what I've been doing wrong. All I know is that wanting hasn't been enough so far. Speaking of my grandmother I was raised by her. When I was born my mother decided she didn't want to be a mother after all and she took off for parts unknown.

I never knew my father either. He was eaten by sharks. Every time I tell that to someone about my father they accuse me of making it up like they do when I say my landlord's name is Raymond Schmuck. How could you make up either one of those things? They're too absurd for fiction. They have to be true. It happened on their honeymoon while my dad was scuba diving. He cut himself on some coral, and the blood attracted a couple of man-eaters. It's hard to miss someone you never knew, but I do wonder about him sometimes, and when I look at his picture I always think of those sharks and hope he died quickly. Given my mother's aversion to motherhood I can only conclude I was an accident. My grandmother never wanted to talk about it. She'd always say what difference does it make?

My interview with Manny wasn't really an interview, since he'd obviously decided on the basis of our telephone conversation that I had the job. He was dark and pudgy, and he wore a diamond pinky ring. Talk about straight out of Central Casting. He studied the application I'd filled out. "How long have you known Trini?"

"A couple of years. We used to work together."

"She's quite a gal."

"She is."

"What do you know about the job?"

"Just what Trini told me."

He put aside the application. "Well let me tell you that Talk To Me is several cuts above the other outfits in this business, and it's because I hire only good people, people who give good voice, and I'm not trying to be funny. We attract the consumer who doesn't mind paying a little more for better product. A good percentage of our business comes from regulars. We accept all major credit cards."

"What if they don't have one?"

"You hang up on the fucker. We cater to straight and gay in both sexes. We also do some specialties."

"Such as?"

"The usual stuff, bondage, threesomes, foursomes."

"How do you do that?"

"What, the group stuff? What do you think a conference line is for? Of course they pay more for that."

"I'm not sure I'd be very good at things that are outside of my frame of reference."

"Don't worry about it. Everyone here finds their own niche. You'll train by listening for a couple of days here at the office. Then we'll set you up in your apartment or wherever the hell you live, and you can work at home. You should have the routine down by the time you go solo, and it is a routine. There are a lot of lonely people out there, people who're looking for something more than a quick come all by themselves. They want to share it with someone that way for a lot of reasons, they think they're ugly or they're scared of catching something or, let's face it, they just like to come over the phone. There's a need and we fill it. Women tend to talk longer than men, and they don't like to start off sexy, you have to ease into it. The regulars are in the file, of course, along with what they like and don't like. You get a commission on your volume, so the incentive is there to keep them on the wire. We've got some regulars, guys mostly, but there're a few women, who like quickies. They're on and off in a minute. It's all in the computer under their name. Any questions?"

I had a lot of questions, but I figured I'd find out the answers better by keeping quiet and observing. As my grandmother used to say, a still tongue makes a wise head.

Manny took me into the training room. There were two small soundproof cubicles with half glass partitions. Each cubicle had a small desk, a chair, a computer, and a telephone. An attractive woman wearing a headset was talking behind the closed door of one. The other one, door open, was occupied by a

15

guy who was reading a magazine with his feet up on the desk. Manny introduced us.

"James is one of my top grossers," he said as James and I shook hands. "James, introduce Marcie when she gets off the line." He squeezed my bicep. "Call me tonight, and we'll talk about your schedule." He waved at Marcie who waved back without smiling. James opened a folding chair and placed it beside the desk. "I used to be the top grosser," he said, "but I got cast in a show that runs Thursday Friday and Saturday which as you may know are the busiest days in the phone sex business."

"I didn't know."

"This is your first job?"

"Yes."

"You'll catch on fast."

"Everyone seems to thinks so."

The phone rang.

"Close the door," said James. "I'll turn on the conference line."

I had to lift the chair in order to get the door closed.

"Hi," said a woman's voice. "Who's this?"

"This is Paul," said James. He had taken his voice down an octave and he talked softly. "Who's this?"

"Darlene."

"What's your credit card number, Darlene?" He keyed the numbers into the computer as she called them. "Just hold on a second, Darlene, while I get an authorization. There. Ok. Where are you calling from, Darlene?"

"My house."

"What are ya doin'?"

"Just laying around. What are you doing?"

"Just laying around, too, waiting for someone to ring my chimes."

She laughed.

"Have you ever called before, Darlene?"

"No, why?"

"Just wondering." He keyed some more numbers into the computer and watched the screen. He looked at me and shook his head no. "What do you look like, Darlene?"

"I'm average height, brown hair, streaked, blue eyes."

"Do you have a nice figure?"

"I could have if I stayed on the plan I'm enrolled in, but it's hard."

"Your voice gets me hard, Darlene."

"Oh, come on."

"I'm not kidding. What are you wearing?"

"Shorts and a halter. I'm out by the pool."

"Can anyone see you?"

"What do you mean? Like the neighbors?"

"Yeah."

"No, it's secluded."

"I'd like to be there with you, Darlene."

"I'm sure."

"I really would. We could go skinny dipping. Do you ever do that?"

"Yes."

"I love the way the water feels on my skin, especially around my cock."

"It's nice." There was a sipping sound and the clink of ice cubes. "What do you look like?"

"I'm tall," said James, "and I've got brown hair. I'm told I look like a young Alex Trebek."

"Who?"

"Alex Trebek. You know, the guy on Jeopardy."

"Oh yeah." Again the sound of ice cubes clinking.

"Do you have a mustache?"

"Do you like mustaches?"

"Sometimes."

"Would you like me to have one?"

"No."

"I shaved if off this morning." He smiled at me while he said it. Actually he was on the short side with blond hair and no mustache. He was so clean cut that I was finding it difficult to believe the sleaze that was coming out of him. He went on. "If I were there with you, Darlene, what would you like to do?"

"Dance."

"By the pool?"

"Yeah."

"Let's do it. Let's take off our clothes and do it."

"I'd feel silly."

"Come on. You said no one can see you. I'm taking off my shoes and socks now."

"I was barefoot when I called."

"I'm slipping off my shirt. Take off your top. I'll help you."

There was a pause. "Ok. It's off."

"Isn't that nice? Doesn't the sun feel good on your breasts?"

"Yes."

"That's me touching them, very lightly, just like the sunlight, barely touching your nipples with my finger tips."

"Yes."

"Touch my nipples," said James.

"Yes."

"Lick them."

"Yes."

"I'm taking off my pants."

"Um."

"I go commando," said James.

"What?"

"I'm not wearing any underwear."

"Um."

"Take off your shorts, Darlene. Take off your panties, too."

"I'm wearing a thong."

"You're killing me, Darlene."

There was another pause. "Ok."

"Are you naked?"

Yes."

"So am I," said James. "God, it's so nice, isn't it?"

"Yes."

"Now let's dance."

"What about the music?'

"Do you have a radio?"

"It's in the house."

"I'll hum. What kind of music do you like?"

"Patsy Cline."

"He started humming Crazy. When he finished he whispered, "Do you have something by the pool to lie on?"

"A mat."

"Good. Let's lie down." He waited. "Ok?"

"Um."

"Are you wet yet?"

"Um."

"Are you?"

"Yes."

"Say it."

"I'm wet."

"Do you want me inside you?"

"Um."

"Say it."

"Be inside me."

"Oh, Darlene, you're so nice, you're so nice." He was whispering now, staring up at the ceiling, oblivious to me. "So, so nice. Are you close?"

"Um."

"Tell me when." He waited for what seemed like a minute. "Darlene?"

"Um."

"Soon now, Darlene, soon."

"Oh."

"Yes, Darlene baby, yes."

"Oh."

"Darlene, come baby, come. Darlene. Now."

"Now, oh, oh, oh, ahhhhh!"

There was another long pause, then the sound of someone moving.

"Darlene?"

"Yes."

"Was it as nice for you as it was for me?"

"Yes."

"Do you want to talk some more?"

"I have to go now."

"Ok, Darlene. Call me again. Ask for Paul."

"Yeah, ok. Bye."

The sound of the dial tone filled the room. James switched it off. "The whole trick," he said, "is setting the scene. Ask a few questions and you can pretty much figure out what they want. That one is a fairly typical daytime call, bored housewife, divorced or neglected by the husband, having a few drinks by the pool if she's lucky enough to have a pool."

I wanted to ask James how this kind of work

affected his personal life, but I can't stand people who get personal with you before they know you well. As I was leaving, Marcie came out of her cubicle. James introduced us. Marcie thought she knew me from somewhere, but I was sure we'd never met. I would have remembered. They both wished me good luck.

Everyone was right. I caught on fast. By the end of three days I knew how to do it, and by the end of my first year, I'm in my second now, I was the top grosser. For the first time in my life I had money in the bank. My rent was paid on the first of every month, and I never had to mix with Schmuck except to nod at him if I saw him around. I had a new car, and my credit cards were almost paid off. My teeth were fixed, and I was even thinking about having the front ones capped. My grandmother used to say that money can't buy happiness, but if she were alive I'd send her a few bucks, so she could see for herself how not having to worry about making ends meet, something she did all her life, is very nice even if it isn't exactly happiness. I mean I can eat out as often as I want. I have state of the art sound , and if I'm shopping and I can't decide what color of something to buy I can buy it in two or even three colors. I can afford to go to a ballgame anytime I want to, and I just bought a computerized exercise bike. Hey, Gram, you've got to admit that's getting up there on the ladder to enjoyment.

But nothing's perfect. To be honest the job can

really get to you. Not wanting to tell people what you do is only part of it. The truth is you feel used, and that affects other aspects of your life. I wondered about it that first day with James. Now I know. When I started working for Manny I was seeing a lady I knew from acting school in New York. She moved out here about the same time I did. We had a pretty good thing going. Her name was Robin, and I say, was, because we're history now. It started falling apart right after I went to work for Manny. I had to tell her what was going on when I started to pay my bills. I suppose I could have told her I was a waiter or something, but when lying is part of your job you need some relief from it somewhere. So I told her. She didn't believe me until I showed her the ad for Talk To Me in one of the free newspapers. We had eaten dinner at her place, and I was planning to spend the night. After dinner we did the dishes and watched the news. In bed when I moved to make love to her she stiffened in my arms and said she just couldn't. I asked her if she wanted to talk, and she said she didn't think it would do any good. I offered to quit the job, but she said she thought it was too late. Her estimation of me had shifted. I love that, her estimation of me.

After that I tried going out with two more women, but it didn't work. I told one of them what I did for a living, and she begged me to call her up and talk dirty to her. That really turned me off. The other one whom I didn't tell had just broken up with a guy who didn't tell her he was married. One thing she didn't need as more deception from men, so I dropped her. I suppose I could have quit the job. I thought about it a lot, but I didn't do it. When you've been poor all your life, and you suddenly strike it rich you don't go back to being poor easily. I normally don't tell people this, but I grew up on welfare. My grandmother was too old to get a job, and besides she had to take care of me.

Being poor is a lot of shitty little things. There's the embarrassment of having to use food stamps for one thing. I'll never forget the time I was in line at the supermarket and ran into Ruthie McCoy, a girl I liked. I was in the seventh grade at the time. We made small talk as we waited our turn. I was dreading having her see me pay with stamps. When it was almost my turn I excused myself saying I'd forgotten something. I told her to go ahead. She offered to wait for me, but I said I had my bike outside. My bike. What a laugh. We had to scrimp to buy the roller skates I got for Christmas that year. Another time when things were tight my grandmother had to rent out my room. The woman who took it fell asleep smoking in bed and set the mattress on fire. We had to call the fire department, and there was a lot of smoke damage and of course an article in the goddamn nosey local newspaper that identified the smoker as a roomer. I was in junior high, and I suppose I shouldn't have been embarrassed, but I was. In addition to my hatred of poverty, another thing that kept me going at Talk To Me was the hope that I'd be cast in something that would start me on my way as a working actor, but it wasn't happening. I went on a lot of auditions, but whatever it was they were looking for I didn't seem to have.

Then Trini came to the rescue again. She called me two days after New Year's. I hadn't seen much of her since I started working for Manny. She was at the office Christmas party, but we didn't get a chance to talk, because she had to play hostess. When we did see each other we would talk about getting together for lunch, but it never happened. If I ate lunch with everyone in this town who said to me, let's have lunch, I'd be going up for fat man roles by now. Instead of so long it was nice to see you people out here say let's have lunch. It's another thing I can't stand about Hollywood. Anyway, Trini really wanted to have lunch so we made a date.

"I quit the job at the agency," she said, as she handed back the menu to the waitress. "Manny just didn't want me to work. That was six months ago, and I'm climbing the walls. Jesus, how do people do nothing all day? I've been taking an acting class, and my teacher says I've definitely got it, but I'm tired of class. I want to do something in front of a real audience."

"Don't we all."

25

"That's what I want to talk about. Manny has agreed to finance a play with me in it. I'm calling him the producer, but he's not going to do anything but sign the checks. I've got another guy to do the real work. We're negotiating for a theater on Melrose, and as we speak it looks like we'll get it. Do you remember, Bucky, the guy from the ribs place?"

I wasn't sure.

"He used to fill in on the grill when Leroy got drunk. Then he took over full time just before the place burned down."

I remembered.

"Bucky's a director in real life. He's been doing children's theater somewhere in the ghetto. He's going to do my show."

"What are you planning on doing?"

"Sweet Bird of Youth, with me as Alexandra Del Lago."

I took a sip of apple juice. "Aren't you a little young for that?"

"You've heard of make-up, I presume. Also I'm going platinum blond which will age me a little more I think. Anyway as long as I look older than the guy who plays Chance Wayne it'll be OK."

"Who's playing Chance Wayne?"

"You, I hope."

"I don't look younger than you."

"I told you I'm going to go platinum. Believe me it adds five years. Jesus, do you want the part or don't you?"

"Yes, I want it."

I immediately went by the office and left a note on Manny's desk giving him a week's notice. I told him I wanted to put all my energy into the play and I was sure he'd understand. I would have to cut back on a few luxuries since I'd only be making union minimum. I figured it wouldn't be for long, because the exposure would generate more work for me possibly even a commercial for network TV.

At Talk To Me I immediately started phasing out my regulars, trying to get them hooked up with someone else in the place. A regular considers you someone with whom he or she has a relationship, like with a counselor, a confident, even a friend. It's kind of sad, really, them having to pay for friendship, and even though I do it for the money I feel some responsibility. I mean I just can't abandon them. That's the problem, most of them have been abandoned too many times already. I like regulars, because they rarely put sexual demands on you. It's the one-time caller who wants sex. I do it of course, because it's part of the job, but I prefer it when they don't want to come. Most of my clients are women, since I work straight, but I have a couple of guys who like to talk about women or to hear me talk about them. Talking dirty with me seems to be as close as they want to get to having sex with a man. So be it. How people get off is their own affair. It's not for me to judge. As long as no one gets hurt and the credit card clears what difference does it make? James, the guy who trained me, works both sides of the street. My regulars run the gamut, married, single, widowed, divorced. The one thing they have in common is no romance in their lives.

Take Florence. She's a waitress in a twenty-four hour coffee shop in North Hollywood. Her big treat every week, usually Thursdays, is to come home from work a little before midnight, have a bath and then call me. I'd guess based on the references she makes that she's in her late fifties. She talks about a boyfriend she never got over who was killed in the Korean War. We do a thing where we talk about a trip we're going to take together up the coast to San Francisco. We've been talking about it for six months now, how we'll drive up the coast, spend the night in Carmel, do Monterey, and finally arrive in San Francisco in the late afternoon. We'll check into the Fairmont Hotel where we'll have a shower together in one of those big elegant tile bathrooms. Then we'll go upstairs to the Crown Room for drinks and watch the sunset. We've even talked about the kind of drinks we'll have, a stinger for her and a Manhattan for me, and how the Golden Gate Bridge will look against the orange sky. I like to think that all the planning will push her into meeting someone and taking the trip for real, but so far it hasn't happened.

"What am I going to do with these clippings?

she asked when I told her I was leaving. She was always cutting out articles about San Francisco.

"You could save them. And speaking of saving, you could start saving the money you spend on these calls towards a real trip." Manny wouldn't like that, but fuck it.

"Isn't ours a real trip?"

"Yes and no."

"It's kept me going, you know. It ain't easy waiting on tables. You put up with a lot of shit for that tip. Every time it gets rough I think about our trip. Joe, couldn't we get together for coffee or something?"

Joe is my telephone name. I told her I was leaving to go back home.

"Where's home?"

"A little town in Mississippi, on the Gulf Coast."

"I didn't know you were from Mississippi. You don't have an accent."

"I've been out here a long time. I lost it."

She started to cry. I asked her if she wanted the name of another guy to call. She said she'd think about it. I told her to take care of herself.

Doing the play was a good experience for me personally, all things considered. I made a giant leap forward as an actor. Chance Wayne is a whore. I know all about him. I'm not saying I didn't have to work hard at it, but the Chance Wayne I showed the audience was entirely believable, if I do say so myself. Not everyone thought so. The guy from the Times said that I'm no Paul Newman. Who for chrissake is? Critics. Marcie, the lady James introduced me to that first day at Talk To Me, was cast as Heavenly Finley the woman Chance loves. Life can imitate art, so to speak, and we started seeing each other off stage.

On stage things didn't go well with the rest of the production. Three days into rehearsal the actor who was playing Boss Finley had a gall bladder attack and had to be hospitalized for surgery. He was replaced by a friend of Manny's, a former radio actor from Teheran. Aside from his Persian accent the replacement lacked the frame of reference he needed to portray a political boss from the Mississippi Delta and he never really got into the part.

The biggest problem, however, turned out to be Trini. I don't know where she got the idea, maybe it was the platinum dye job, but she apparently made the decision to imitate Marilyn Monroe. Bucky was driven to distraction. Trini didn't understand that an actor, especially an inexperienced one, is better off trusting the director. She fought Bucky at every turn. She insisted on speaking in a whispery voice, she twitched her lips after every speech, and she flashed her tits every chance she got. A week before we opened she fired Bucky, and Manny came on as director. Marcie and I considered walking, but we decided to be professional and see it through to the end.

We lasted for five performances. Most of our

audiences were Persian friends of Manny's who tended to be noisy even though they seem to enjoy themselves. We always got enthusiastic applause at the curtain call. I see no point in further quoting the critics. The exposure didn't lead to any more acting work, let alone a network TV commercial, and I went back to work at Talk To Me.

I'm saving up now to move back to New York. Hollywood just isn't my town. Marcie is working at Borders. We don't see each other anymore. She wanted to put phone work behind her, and she couldn't deal with my staying with it. She's lived in New York and knows that being poor there isn't pretty, but I couldn't convince her. The job isn't easy as I've said many times, but it isn't forever. If you can see the light at the end of the tunnel you can always keep going. In the play, Chance Wayne has a speech where he says if he gave up hope he'd just have to swim out to sea until the sharks took him for live bait. Live bait. It always made me think of my dad.

WHERE THE HEART IS

Eduardo Veracruz put down the skin magazine he was looking at and laid back on his bed, a mattress on the floor in the corner of the room that was his home. He hardly ever bought a magazine, let alone such a one as this, pictures of men and women having sex, sometimes three at a time. This one he bought last week in the early hours of the morning on his way home from his job, one of three jobs he had, as a valet car park in a restaurant on Doheny in Beverly Hills. The restaurant served Russian food, whatever that was, and called itself a tea room. It was just another confusing thing among hundreds of confusing things in this city that was more like a brightly lit dream than a city, a place with no boundaries, no rhythm, no center to hold it together.

The magazine had lain on the floor beside the mattress ever since he dropped it there that night, too tired to look at it. He had been on his feet since dawn, first delivering newspapers with his friend Jaime in Jaime's truck and then bussing tables at The Better Burrito on Pico near the Fox movie studios. Today was his day off from bussing tables and after he and Jaime, newspapers delivered, had coffee and a hot dog at Pink's he came home and slept until the clock buzzed to tell him it was time to get ready to park cars.

Only it wasn't time. He had set the clock wrong. He could lie in bed another hour if he wanted to. It was then that he glanced at the magazine there on the floor and picked it up. Now, he stared at the tent his stiff *pinga* had created in the sheet. The magazine had done its work, no doubt about that. He touched himself and thought about his wife in El Salvador, how warm her body was in the night, how good she smelled. He came very quickly. He was twenty-two years old, and it was a year since he left his village fleeing the army recruiter, his wife in tears, their infant daughter wailing as if she knew what was going on.

On the way down the hall to the bathroom he passed Hendel's room. He could hear the old man inching toward the door with his walker. Moving like a giant sea turtle, Hendel took almost two hours to shuffle down the long hallway to the mailbox and back to the metal folding chair next to the card table in his room. Except for this walk he spent most of the day in that chair listening to a squawky little radio that sat on the table. Some days he would sit on the front steps for a while, always the middle step, enjoying the sun. His legs, in metal braces, lay in front of him like two poles. Once a month he would visit the doctor and go to the bank, a project involving taxi cabs that took all day.

Eduardo turned off the shower and dried

himself quickly. He pulled on his trousers and cracked the bathroom door, peeking out into the hallway to check where Hendel was. The old man had made it as far as the doorway of his room where he stood now, pushing the walker ahead of himself through the doorframe. There was no way to avoid him.

"*Buenos dias, senor.*"

"*Buenos dias,* Eduardo!"

Eduardo unlocked the door to his room. "*Como esta?*"

"Wonderful!" said Hendel. He always made it sound like he was cheering at a cockfight.

"Shall I get the mail for you?"

"No," said Hendel, "but there is something you could do."

There was always something. "I must go to work now, *senor,* but sometime over the weekend I will come to your room."

"I need razor blades," said Hendel. "Let me give you the money." He pulled from his pocket a ten dollar bill wrapped in a piece of paper.

Eduardo took it. "I will get them tomorrow."

"Good, good. Also there's a coupon for fifty cents off. Get those kind, on the coupon."

"Tomorrow, *senor.*"

"*Muchos gracias!*"

Eduardo closed the door. Hendel's enthusiasm annoyed him. How could it be wonderful with no

family or friends, the lower half of your body dead, your world a smelly room crowded with boxes and dusty books with gray dirty sheets on the narrow bed? They had met the day Eduardo moved in. Hendel's door was open, and, sitting in his folding chair, he watched Eduardo and Jaime bring in the mattress and some boxes with household stuff Jaime's wife had rounded up. It was a hot day, and Eduardo, too, left his door open while he set up the hot plate, put away the few dishes and pans and made up the bed. Hendel, on the way to the mailbox, stopped at Eduardo's doorway. "Does this
room have a toilet?" he asked.

"Pardon, *senor*?"

"A toilet! A toilet! Does this room have a toilet!"

"Ah, no. It is there, across the hall."

"I know that, but some rooms have their own toilets. Mine has a toilet and a sink, but no bathtub."

"I have a sink."

Satisfied, Hendel resumed his journey. By the time Eduardo was leaving for work the old man had gotten his mail, now in a plastic bag attached to the walker, and was halfway back to his room. "You don't have parties!"

"No, *senor*."

Parties. Eduardo had forgotten what a party was. Once in a while, on Saturday nights after parking cars, he went with Jaime to a club on Olivera Street where the Salvadorans hung out. He didn't go often, because you had to buy a round when it was your turn, and that could add up. Also, the women tempted him, and if you danced with them you had to buy them a drink, too. He was trying to save to bring his wife and daughter here. Jaime's cousin knew a man who, for five thousand dollars, could get her, without the baby, to Tijuana. From there she could be smuggled, like a piece of furniture, into Los Angeles. The price included someone with papers who would bring the baby in later, once they were settled.

It was hard to save. His rent, food, and what he sent to his wife took most of what he made. So far, he had just over a thousand dollars hidden under the mattress. He didn't like to think about how long it would take him to get five thousand. Eduardo himself, after making his way north to Mexico, came in as a migrant to work in the fields. One night, on the way to the showers, he started running. In his pocket he had the name of a Salvadoran priest in Bakersfield who was known to help people. He never found the priest. He never even got to Bakersfield. Instead he was picked up by a crazy gringo kid who was taking a lot of little blue pills. The kid got so stoned Eduardo had to drive. With the kid passed out in the back seat, Eduardo wearing the kid's San Francisco Giants baseball cap so he would look less suspicious behind the wheel followed the freeway signs right into downtown Los Angles. When they said goodbye the kid forgot to ask for his cap back.

Eduardo still had it.

Work that night was like he was afraid hell would be. Normally there were six of them parking cars, but two guys, Nicaraguans, got picked up by Immigration, and four had to do the work of six. The senior guy, Juanito, a Mexican, said it was Nicaraguan stupidity that got them arrested, but Aurelio, also a Nicaraguan, told Eduardo that it was Juanito's fault, because he had taken money to get them fake green cards and couldn't deliver on time. Juanito's cousin, who was supposed to get the green cards, was jailed for beating his wife, and the Nicaraguans, said Aurelio, had to take the blame. Jaime had gotten Eduardo's green card from a guy in Long Beach who said he was a lawyer. It cost Eduardo a thousand dollars.

All that night parking cars Juanito screamed at them in order to get the heat from the angry customers off himself. Eduardo couldn't understand these people. They would pay a fortune for their food, Aurelio told him it could cost over three hundred dollars for two people to eat there, take sometimes four hours to eat it, and then jump up and down if they had to wait fifteen minutes for their cars. Once Eduardo, hurrying to bring a car around, got into the wrong one. While he was trying to get the key into the ignition where it wouldn't fit he became aware of someone in the back seat and smelled perfume in the dark. He turned to see a woman with a coke spoon at her nose. He bolted from the car before she could say anything. When the night was over his shirt was soaked with sweat. They did very well on tips, splitting four ways instead of six, but he wasn't sure it was worth it. Aurelio, who drove Eduardo home, wanted to go drinking, but Eduardo wanted only sleep.

The next morning he waited at dawn for Jaime to pick him up to deliver newspapers in Silver Lake. As he locked the door of his room he saw the light coming from under Hendel's door and he heard the old man singing along with the scratchy opera music that came from his small radio. Hendel told Eduardo that he had studied opera, that once he had sung in the opera house in Buenos Aires. Eduardo was curious to hear more about this, but Hendel rationed out what he told about himself, and Eduardo, who was used to people not talking about their pasts, didn't push it. Once while they sat together on the front steps, it was Sunday and Eduardo had the night off, Hendel rolled up his sleeve and showed Eduardo a tattoo of numbers on his arm. He asked Eduardo if he knew what they were. Eduardo said they looked like numbers. Hendel got very upset and asked Eduardo if he knew any Jews. Eduardo didn't. He had heard about them in church, of course, that they killed Jesus on the cross. Then all that changed. One day, Eduardo was maybe eight years old at the time and still going with his mother to Mass, the priest read a letter from the bishop telling them that the Jews were not responsible for killing Jesus. After Mass Eduardo asked his mother who did it if it wasn't the Jews? She didn't know either. Soon after that he stopped going to church altogether, and he forgot about the whole thing. He told none of this to Hendel who showed no interest in Eduardo's life anyway. Once Eduardo showed Hendel a picture of his baby daughter, and the old man hardly looked at it.

Hendel lived only for himself, spending a lot of his time arranging for others, especially Eduardo these days, to do things for him that he couldn't do for himself which was mostly everything. He got his food from something called Meals On Wheels, but he always needed stuff from the drugstore or the Seven Eleven. Eduardo wondered who shopped for Hendel before he came along. Who reached up to bring things down from the top shelf? Who cleared the drain in the dirty little sink in Hendel's bathroom when it was clogged with oatmeal? Who, when he answered the old man's shouts one day, went to his room to find him on the toilet, shit stinking up the place, got him a roll of toilet paper from the box under the bed?

He finally found out about the numbers on Hendel's arm. It was a night he had taken off, his birthday, and Jaime's wife had cooked a meal for him.

There had been mescal and beer, and he was a

little drunk when he came home and more than a little sad. He ached for his wife and child. That morning he had counted the money under the mattress and found that it had grown very little since he last time he counted. Handel's door was open, and the radio was playing the classical music he always listened to, something that sounded Spanish. Jaime's wife had given Eduardo some flan to take home, and he decided to bring it to Hendel. The old man, seated in the metal chair, was dozing when Eduardo knocked on the doorframe. Hendel accepted the flan and told Eduardo to get him a spoon from a shelf in the bathroom. He hated Hendel's bathroom. While the old man ate Eduardo waited for him to ask where the flan came from, and why was Eduardo wearing a new white shirt? Hendel didn't ask. Instead, he talked about a letter he had received that day, a letter from his son in Israel. This was the first time Eduardo had ever heard Hendel mention a family. He had only one picture on his wall, of himself as a young man wearing a coat and necktie, his hair black and slick. Looking at the picture Eduardo wondered if he had the use of his legs when it was taken.

"Do you believe in God?" asked Hendel.

"Yes, *senor*."

"You are a fool."

"Pardon?"

"You're a fool, like him." He pointed to the letter lying on the table.

Eduardo didn't know what to say.

"He's like his mother," said Hendel, eyes on the letter. "She and her crazy brothers, full of Talmud and Zion and all the craziness that keeps people in ignorance and superstition."

"I do not understand, *senor.*"

"What are you, Catholic?'

"Yes."

"Do you know what happened to the Jews while the Pope was occupied with other things?"

Eduardo was beginning to think Hendel might be a little drunk too.

"While the Pope was making pacts with the Fascists six million people were murdered."

"Was this a war, *senor?*"

"Yes, yes it was a war." Hendel waved his hand in front of his face as if there was a fly buzzing there.

"I know about war," said Eduardo.

"What do you know?"

He told Hendel about how the rebel fighters came to the village. They wanted food. They told the people that there would be land for everyone when the revolution came, but for now they must help the fight by giving them food. The people gave. Then the government soldiers came. They shot four men right there in front of the church. They said the men were Communists. One of those shot was Eduardo's brother, a school teacher. After that it was death squads pounding on doors in the night, gun shots, wailing women, torture. The torture was the worst part. He started to tell about the torture, but he stopped. Hendel wasn't listening.

"They took all of us," said Hendel. "I was a music student, my sisters were dancers. My father and mother were musicians. They cared nothing about politics. My father was a freethinker, tied to no dogma or superstition, but the Nazis didn't care about that. A Jew was a Jew."

"Did they kill your father?"

"THEY PUT HIM IN THE OVENS!"

The shout made Eduardo jump, and then he pictured a man baking in the oven like a loaf of bread, and he felt his stomach turn. He wanted to get out of Hendel's room fast. "I am sorry, *senor.*"

Hendel thrust his arm forward. "And they marked us with numbers. The mohels marked us with their knives and the Nazis with their tattoo needles!" He lowered his arm and stared at Eduardo. "And you believe in God." He almost whispered it.

"Yes."

"You are a fool."

The next morning on their newspaper route the clutch on Jaime's truck started slipping. Besides delivering newspapers in it he used it to haul furniture. On Sundays after driving all night to get it from up north he sold produce from its back at a farmers market in San Fernando.

"Come on, you son of a bitch," said Jaime

hitting the steering wheel with the back of his hand. "Don't die on me now."

Jaime had five kids and another one on the way. He told Eduardo that his wife said he had to use condoms after the baby was born. While they did the route Eduardo thought about his own wife. She wrote him a letter every week to tell him about their daughter and to thank him for the money he sent. They had been married for only a year when he left. She kept asking him when he would have enough money to bring her north, and he always lied, telling her a couple of months more. At the rate he was saving it would be more like a couple of years. She told him she was afraid he would get another woman. Some men did that, even going so far as to marry the second one and have children while the first one waited far away with the ones he had made with her. He would never do that to his wife. She was the most beautiful of all the young women in the village, and he still smiled when he thought of how she chose him over all the others she could have had.

When they finished the route Jaime dropped him off at The Better Burrito. The clutch was slipping badly now. Jaime was going to have to take it to a mechanic.

"I'll see you tomorrow," he said, "unless this motherfucker is in pieces on the floor of the garage."

Eduardo entered the kitchen through the restaurant's back door and went to his locker in the supply pantry where he changed into his black trousers. Carrying a clean white shirt, a towel, and a deodorant stick he went into the men's room and washed. Feeling clean again he joined the other busboys, Jesus and Carlos, at the serving station. As usual Carlos was complaining about having to clean up after the busboys who worked the night shift. Jesus, his partner, kept saying, "I know, I know." They were small men, Puerto Rican. Eduardo thought they looked like teen age boys. He had been surprised to learn that they were almost thirty. They had come here from New York hoping to make a CD, but when they got here the guy who was supposed to be their agent, and who took a deposit on their future earnings, had disappeared. Jesus played the guitar and Carlos the marimba. Carlos also sang. They had night jobs in a gay restaurant on La Cienega, and occasionally, Carlos told Eduardo, they turned a trick. But only as a team, he said. Eduardo's older cousin who lived in Miami did that too, turned tricks. One Christmas when he was home the cousin, wearing alligator shoes and a gold watch, told Eduardo that he could do it too. His cousin said that the men were rich, generous, and for the most part easy to please. It was before Eduardo got married and before he heard of AIDS, and tired of being poor, he was tempted. Eduardo, said his cousin, had the looks for the job. It didn't mean he was gay just because the men were.

"You are gay?" asked Eduardo.

"A little bit," said his cousin.

Eduardo thought about it but decided it wasn't for him although once in a while when he thought of Jesus and Carlos he couldn't help being curious about what they did together and who did what.

The waiters arrived and immediately started arguing about what station they were supposed to have. All of them were actors who couldn't find acting jobs, and they could be hard to work with sometimes. The busboy went with the station, and they all wanted Eduardo's, because he was the fastest. Jesus was only OK, and Carlos was the slowest. He was also moody and easily wounded. Harry, a big good-looking black guy, lost his temper one day out on the floor, and calling Carlos, needledick, told him to move his little ass faster.

"To think he would say that in front of the customers," Carlos sobbed in the panty. "I suppose his is like a fire hose."

"I know, I know," said Jesus.

Today Eduardo worked with Steven, a redheaded guy who wanted to make a living telling jokes in nightclubs. Now, he did this for free at a place up on Sunset, but someday, he told Eduardo, he hoped to do it in Las Vegas and Atlantic City where you could make ten or twenty thousand a week. Eduardo liked to work with Steven, because he was a good waiter and because he never short-changed his busboy when it came to turning over a share of the tips. Most of the other waiters did that, pretending they took in less than they did, and there was nothing a busboy could do about it. No one forced the waiters to show their money. You had to take their word for it. Eduardo's father told him long ago not to expect the world to be fair, and he had seen nothing so far to prove his father wrong.

During lunch Carlos knocked over a pitcher of ice water into the lap of a fat lady who was a regular customer and very picky. It was busy with people waiting for tables, and the commotion of stripping and re-setting the table, re-ordering the food, and calming down the fat lady with dry towels and a free glass of wine did not go down well with the manager. Jesus, who was working with Harry, abandoned his station to come to the aid of Carlos who looked like he was going to burst into tears. He cries too easily, thought Eduardo. Harry yelled at Jesus to get back to his own station, Steven told Harry to calm down, and the manager, who was normally very easy-going, fired Carlos, who let out a sob and ran off the floor. Eduardo and Jesus had to split the station Carlos abandoned while they continued to cover their own. Jesus kept mumbling that he would have to quit. Eduardo begged him to wait until lunch was over.

By the time they closed at three o'clock Carlos had been re-hired. He and the manager had a conference, and when the manager learned that he was going to lose Jesus too, he reconsidered. In the pantry, Carlos, tears forgotten and cocky now, sat on a sack of rice and smoked a cigarette while he waited for Jesus to change his clothes.

"You'd think she never got her pussy wet before," he said.

"I know," said Jesus.

Before he went to park cars that night Eduardo brought the razor blades to Hendel. He watched Hendel count the change. The old man was very tight with money. He told Eduardo he was retired from a studio job with a small pension. From the way he lived it looked like it wasn't much. Tonight Hendel seemed tired and his face was gray. Eduardo offered to heat up some soup for him, but Hendel said, no, he would eat a peanut butter sandwich. These gringos and their peanut butter, thought Eduardo. Even Jaime's kids ate it.

That night he dreamed his wife wrote a letter telling him their daughter was going to get married. In the dream he was on the phone trying to tell her that a baby couldn't get married, but it was a bad connection, and he couldn't make her understand. He was starting to panic when he woke up to see the room flooded in a flickering red light coming from behind the shade in the front window. He heard voices in the hall followed by a knock on his door. He opened it to see two men.

"Hendel?" asked one of the men.

"There." Eduardo pointed to the door across the hall. He grabbed his trousers and pulled them on quickly. The men were pounding on Hendel's door when he joined them. There was no answer.

"Who called you?" asked Eduardo.

"It was a 911," said one of the men, a Chinese guy. "He must have done it himself."

The other guy took a pick from his pocket and started on the lock. It opened right away. When they entered the room Hendel was lying on the floor next to the metal chair. His eyes were open. The phone, off the hook, lay beside him, a beeping noise coming out of it. The radio was playing softly, music. The Chinese guy hung up the phone and put it back on the table while the other guy shone a light into Hendel's eyes. "Can you hear me?" There was no answer. The man squeezed Hendel's wrist while he looked at a watch on his own. Then he listened to Hendel's heart. "Possible stroke," he said to the Chinese guy who was out in the hall unfolding a stretcher.

The Chinese guy pushed the stretcher into the room next to where Hendel lay. Together the men picked up Hendel and put him on the stretcher. Hendel's billfold lay on the table. "Look at that, " said the Chinese guy. "See if there's a Medicare card."There was. "Let's go," he said. Eduardo walked beside the stretcher while he searched Hendel's face. It showed no sign of life except for the eyes. Eduardo thought he saw something in Hendel's eyes like he was trying to say something.

"Where are you taking him?"

"County."

He stood in the dark watching the ambulance drive away. County. What did that mean, county? Jaime would know. Upstairs, in the room over this own, he could see the old lady who lived there looking out the window. He had never seen her outside of that room. Inside, he checked Hendel's door. The men had closed it behind them, but the lock hadn't caught. He went in and turned off the radio. He looked around the room as if for the first time. It was filthy. The Meals On Wheels lady told Hendel that the city would send someone to clean it, but Hendel didn't want that. "Just the food," Eduardo heard him tell the woman, "just the food."

Eduardo wondered why Hendel didn't have shelves for his books. He picked one up. It was in German. Hendel said that was his first language. There was an album of photographs. Eduardo sat on the metal chair to look at the pictures. They were old, none of them in color. There was one of Hendel as a boy, Eduardo had no trouble recognizing him, standing between a man and a woman who must have been his parents. They were all smiling, a large building with a dome in back of them. Hendel's legs had no braces on them, and he wore a long scarf around his neck. Eduardo wondered again, as he had so many times, what happened to Hendel's legs. He opened the closet door. There were a couple of suits hanging there, and on the shelves there were boxes with German words written on them with a marker pen. On the floor were some dirty shirts, a pair of rubber boots with buckles on them, and in the corner, a metal box. Eduardo leaned over to look more closely at the box. He picked it up and set it on the table. It was locked, but the locked could be easily picked. With the box under his arm he turned out the light and left the room, closing the door behind him. The lock caught.

In his own room he sat on the mattress and with a pocket knife forced open the lock on the box. It was full of bills, twenties and hundreds, done up in packets with a rubber band on each. Breathing fast, he dumped the money on his bed and slipped the rubber bands off the packets. Then he realized that the packets probably had the same number of bills. He could have counted the packets first, but it was too late now. His stomach felt like it did when he first looked into the skin magazine. He counted the money twice. Almost twenty thousand dollars. After he counted it the second time he returned the money to the box, closed it, and put it on the closet shelf next to the San Francisco Giants baseball cap. He put the rubber bands into the trash and lay on his bed, hands behind his head, staring up at the ceiling. It was starting to get light outside, and Jaime would be picking him up in less than an hour.

All the time they worked that morning Eduardo wanted to tell Jaime what he found, but Jaime had a way of taking over, and with money like that the fewer hands on it, the better. For the next two days as he went about his jobs he tried not to think about the money. Then he would pass Hendel's door or see the old man's mail stuffed tightly against the opening in the mailbox door, and he would think of the metal box on his closet shelf, and he would get that tickling feeling in his stomach like he did the night he found it. Eduardo knew that if Hendel came back he would have some explaining to do, but that too he put out of his mind. He wasn't sure what he was waiting for. Then, on the fourth day after they took Hendel away Eduardo was coming out of the bathroom when he saw that the old man's door was open. With his heart in his mouth he tapped on the doorframe and entered the room. The landlord was there looking around at the mess. Eduardo asked about Hendel.

"He' dead," said the landlord, "and now I've got to clean up all his shit."

Eduardo crossed himself.

"You want to make some money? I could use some help."

"I must go to my job."

At The Better Burrito he was unable to concentrate. Steven had to keep reminding him to fill the water glasses. He forgot to make coffee, and they ran out, which made Harry mad. Even Carlos made a crack.

"I hate to say anything about Mr. Perfect, but you're fucking up a lot today."

Eduardo's mind was on the letter he would write to his wife when he finished parking cars that night. He would tell her first that the money had been paid, that someone would be in touch with her very soon. Then he would tell her about the place he was getting for them to live in. A large place, it would have three bedrooms, one for them, one for their daughter, and one for the new one they would make as soon as she arrived. They would have a king size bed. She would have a refrigerator and a washing machine with a dryer, and some new dresses. He would tell her about the car he planned to buy, probably a Chevrolet, and mention the beach where you could go to have a picnic on Sundays.

He wrote the letter that night and took it to the post office the next morning. Waiting in line to buy a stamp he stood in back of a man dressed all in black except for his white shirt which was buttoned up to the collar. The man had a bushy black beard and at his ears two long round curls like the kind little girls have for their First Communion. On the floor next to the man was a large box wrapped in heavy paper. Eduardo looked at the address on the box. The word, ISRAEL, jumped out at him, and all of a sudden he thought of Hendel's son, and he stepped out of line and left the post office with the letter to his wife in his pocket. When he got home he put the letter on the floor next to his mattress and wondered what to do next. The money that had come to him from heaven was not from heaven after all. It was Hendel's son's money. Had Hendel told his son about it? What if he hadn't? What if Eduardo was the only one who knew? What if the son's name and address were gone, taken away with all of Hendel's junk that the landlord had put out on the sidewalk for the garbage man? Even if he wanted to turn over the money, who would he give it to? Not the landlord. He would probably keep it, too. Telling the police was out. They would check out his green card.

All that night while he parked cars he thought about the money. When Aurelio suggested that they go for something to eat he was tempted. He hadn't eaten since breakfast, but he said wasn't hungry. That night he got no sleep, and the next day he still couldn't eat anything except a couple of candy bars. To keep the money would be stealing, he finally admitted that to himself, but to give it up was to return to the place where he lived on hope alone. He was afraid that he wasn't strong enough to go back to that place. Finding the money had weakened him. He wanted his wife, his daughter, a home, a life. Another week went by and it got no easier. Jaime asked him if he was ok. "You look like you're losing weight."

The lady was standing on the front steps

looking at the names on the mail boxes when Jaime dropped him off. She asked Eduardo if he lived in the building and if he knew Mr. Hendel. Eduardo told her he did.

The lady gave him a card saying she worked for a lawyer who represented Mr. Hendel's son. The son, said the lady, had reason to believe that his father left some money in the room he lived in. The landlord said he found nothing when he cleaned it. Did Eduardo know anything about it?

"I have the money."

The lady got very flustered. It was clear she hadn't expected this. She asked him where it was. He told her it was in his room, and she followed him there. He had left the window closed, and the room smelled stale. He was ashamed of it, but the woman didn't seem to notice. He took the metal box from the closet shelf, put it on the mattress, and opened it. Her eyes widened.

"How much is there?"

"Almost twenty thousand dollars."

She asked him if he would be willing to turn it over to her. Otherwise, if he wanted, she would get someone from the Sheriff's office to come by and pick it up. Eduardo told her to take the money. The woman said she couldn't speak for Hendel's son, but she would find out if he wanted to reward Eduardo for his honesty.

She wrote down his name and address. When

she left he felt light headed. He lay down on his bed and slept until it was time to park cars.

The Russian place wasn't very busy that night. Eduardo and Aurelio spent a lot of time talking. Aurelio's wife was pregnant with their second child, and he was going to have to get more work. He had applied for a job as a waiter in a Cuban place downtown. He told the manager he had experience which wasn't true. For a reference he gave the name of this brother-in-law who was going to say that he managed a restaurant and that Aurelio had been a good waiter there. Aurelio wasn't worried about being able to do the job. "How hard can it be?" he said.

Later at home, undressing for bed, Eduardo looked at the unstamped letter to his wife lying next to the mattress. He picked it up and put it on the closet shelf where the metal box had been. Someday when they were old he would tell her the story of Hendel's money, and then he would show her the letter. She would read it and know for sure how much he loved her, and how, on that day when she chose him over all of the others, she had chosen well.

STANDING IN FOR LANA
(1947)

I saw them staring at me, as I waited for the clerk to ring up my purchase. They were typical bobby soxers, you saw them around all the time, especially in places like that, a theatrical make-up store at the corner of Gower and Sunset, up the street from Paramount. Always on the lookout for movie stars, most of them carried autograph books in their shoulder bags. I can't deny it I love it when they stare, and like most people who get stared at a lot I've developed the ability to observe them without appearing to notice them. All the stars can do it. It's kind of ironic when you think about it. A star spends his or her life trying to get looked at, and then when they finally succeed they either pretend to hate it or not to care. She claims she doesn't think about it, but you only have to see her, as I did recently, with Tyrone Power in a booth at Musso's, her pot roast untouched, her hair shining like a gold coin in the sunlight, to know that it was there she wanted to be more than anyplace else, doing that, drawing all eyes.

By the time I got my change the bobby soxers had seen that I wasn't her. I saw them laughing about it. It's my nose. It isn't large, but it isn't perfectly shaped like hers is. When people take me for her at first glance it's always my nose that gives me away.

Everything else is similar. I always keep my hair the same shade as hers, it's dark now for Green Dolphin Street, and in the same style. Our figures are practically identical. My job is to fill her space when the focus is on the other actors in a scene, so having a figure like hers is a must. I don't quite have her breasts of course but then, as Harry the guy I was going out with said, who does?

It was the day after New Year's, and I was buying some pancake make-up to replace what I'd lost on New Year's Eve when someone walked off with my clutch which I'd left on the vanity in the ladies room at the Coconut Grove. Harry wanted to raise a stink with the manager, but I said never mind there's only some mad money, a hankie, and the pancake make-up in it. Sometimes Harry got carried away with the Sir Galahad routine. Normally I would have been at the studio instead of shopping for make-up, but we got an unexpected day off when you know who didn't show up on the set that morning. They sent everyone home at noon. No one knew for sure where she was, but I had my ideas. The buzz from upstairs was that Mr. Mayer was foaming at the mouth, but what could he do, really? Green Dolphin Street was too close to a wrap to change stars even if he wanted to which I'm sure he didn't. The grosses from Weekend At the Waldorf and The Postman Always Rings Twice made her Metro's top money earner for the year. She'd get a bawling out, if anything. My job was safe, thank God.

I wasn't sure how much longer Harry would be around, since he'd been talking marriage lately, and I hadn't responded in a way you could call enthusiastic. Harry's an electrician at R.K.O., and that's all he'll ever be. In the looks department he isn't Tyrone Power, let's put it that way. He owns a two family house on Stanley Avenue. His parents live in the ground floor apartment, and Harry has the upstairs. Being married to him would mean living upstairs over his parents, the smell of brisket cooking for the Friday night meal coming through the upstairs kitchen window, my kitchen window, from Harry's mother's kitchen window downstairs. Goodbye Metro Goldwyn Mayer, goodbye Spencer Tracy, she's going to star with him in Cass Timberlaine when she finishes Dolphin Street, and goodbye show business. I got sick when I thought about it.

Being a stand-in isn't exactly the big time, but it's a long way from the corseteria at the May Company. That was my life before I got this job, selling corsets by day and dancing every night at The Hollywood Canteen. I used to get taken for her even in those days. One night she came in with John Hodiak. They were doing a picture together at the time, and I was working hat check. I saw her look at me, not in a hostile way, but interested, like you knew she saw the resemblance. I'd always adored her of course ever since Love Finds Andy Hardy, but it never occurred to me that our paths would ever cross. Later that night I let a soldier take me home. He was a big blond Swede from Wisconsin and a bit on the clumsy side, if you know what I mean. I closed my eyes and pretended he was John Hodiak.

Soon after that I met Harry. His best friend's girlfriend was a secretary in the Casting Department at Metro. One night on a double date she remarked on the resemblance and said I should come in for an interview, because they were looking for a stand-in. I got the job, and a month later I was working on Keep Your Powder Dry. To tell the truth it wasn't quite that simple. I had to maneuver my way across a couple of casting couches, three to be exact, but hey, that's Hollywood. She doesn't remember seeing me at the Canteen. We're not close like some stars and their stand-ins. They say Joan Crawford treats hers like a sister. Don't get me wrong, she's nice enough, but on the set she's all business. And let me tell you she's a cameraman's dream. He never has to worry about focus, because she always hits her key light to perfection. Frankly, I don't think she needs friends. Stars don't seem to. They have hundreds of people catering to their every whim, and they don't have to put themselves out for anyone.

It was getting dark when I came out of the makeup store. I stopped at the market on the way home to pick up a lamb chop for my dinner. The first thing I noticed when I let myself into my apartment was the light on in the place next door. My neighbor was home. He must have gone away for the holiday, because I hadn't seen a light over there for a while. Before I turned on my lights I went into the bedroom and looked out the window. His bedroom window faced mine. He always left his shade up. I put down my packages, took off my coat, and waited. I figured I'd give it five minutes. It was more like ten before he came into the bedroom with his shirt off. He had a torso Victor Mature would envy. That physique was the first thing I noticed about him when he moved in a couple of months ago. He and the fellow who was helping him move worked all day with their shirts off. I've always been a pushover for a set of shoulders. Cowboy handsome, probably an actor, he looked like he was in his late twenties, the perfect age. The only time I ever saw him was like that, through my window, as he moved around his place. We never met on the street. I knew a lot about him, though, including his name, Kenneth Pine. I got that from his mailbox one day when I was sure he was out.

He was vain. He spent a lot of time grooming himself. He had a mirror on the wall of his bedroom that I couldn't see from mine. He'd stand facing it and do the things people, especially beautiful people, do in front of mirrors. He had a hard time making up his mind. Sometimes he'd take a half hour to pick out a shirt. He'd hold up different ones in front of himself as he looked in the mirror. He'd finish buttoning one and then take it off and put on another one. He played tennis every Sunday morning, always leaving the house at ten thirty in his whites. He was fond of the color blue. He wore it a lot, and his bedspread was blue, royal blue. His love life he conducted someplace else. Except for the day he moved in I never saw anyone there.

He cleaned the place himself, usually on Sunday afternoons when he came back from his tennis game. Now, as I waited in the dark, I watched him stand naked looking at himself in the mirror that I couldn't see. He fondled his whatchamacallit the way I've notice a lot of men do when they first get naked, as if to reassure themselves that it hasn't disappeared since the last time they checked. He went to his dresser and took out a pair of shorts before he left the room. He was going to take a shower or a bath, I wondered which. By now my cat, crazy from the smell of raw lamb, was trying to claw open the grocery bag. It was time to get back to the real world. I had a make-up call for seven the next morning.

While the lamb chop was broiling my friend Hortense who works in publicity at the studio called to ask me if I had seen Florabel Muir's column. It seems her nibs had flown off to Mexico to spend New Year's Eve with Tyrone Power who was down there shooting Captain From Castile. The location was quite a ways from Mexico City, and a storm prevented her from getting there in time to make a flight to Los

Angeles that would have gotten her back on time. I knew that's where she went. She's absolutely nuts about Ty Power. I had no sooner hung up from Hortense when Harry called to see if he could come over. I told him I had a headache. Later, before I got into bed, I checked next door. All the windows were dark. He was out for the evening.

She was on the set the next morning, and Green Dolphin Street was wrapped by the end of the next week. Before I knew it we were shooting Cass Timberlaine with Spencer Tracy. It was the happiest set I've ever worked on. Ty Power, back from Mexico, wasn't working, so he was there practically all the time which made her very happy. She never looked better. When's she's in love she glows, and the camera was picking it up. It's a good thing they were shooting me from the back.

My relationship with Harry was headed for the rocks, and it was just a matter of time. It was a shame, because Harry had a lot to offer a woman, as Hortense was always reminding me. I didn't know what I was looking for, but I knew it wasn't Harry. Hortense thought I was crazy. She said she'd give her eyeteeth for a guy with a studio job and a house near Fairfax Avenue. The trouble with Harry, from my point of view, was that he didn't do anything for me, you know, physically. I have to say he was kind and generous and considerate, all the things my mother told me to look for. What she didn't mention was the other stuff. Maybe she didn't care about it, I don't know. I cared about it though, and it had become a sticking point between us although Harry didn't know it. Every time I saw her snuggling up to Tyrone Power I thought of me doing the same thing with Harry and my heart sank.

Then without warning it happened, just like in the movies. Real love came into my life in the form of Kenneth Pine, the guy next door. It was a Saturday, and I was coming home from the pet groomers where I had taken the cat for a flea dip. When I pulled up in front of my place he was there changing a tire on his car. I was wearing shorts and a halter, and I'd been working on my tan. I normally don't get a tan, but she had gone deep sea fishing with Ty and came back with one, so I had no choice. Anyway, I look pretty good in shorts, and I took my time getting out of the car. It's a rare man who can resist the inside of thigh, and Ken was no exception. After we talked for a while he said what everyone says, and I told him I was her stand-in. He was surprised that I lived next door, since he'd never seen me. Imagine. I thought of all the hours I'd spent looking at him. He didn't waste any time, asking me if I wanted to drive out to the beach that night for a fish dinner. I said yes and went right upstairs to call Harry and break my date with him.

I'll remember that night for as long as I live. We drove out to the beach with the top down and had cocktails on a terrace overlooking the ocean. The setting sun was as red as the cherry in my Manhattan. Later there was a full moon, and after dinner we walked on the beach. I was right about him being an actor. He was under contract to Monogram doing walk-ons in low budget westerns, but, he assured me, his sights were on bigger things. On the way home I decided to break my rule about sleeping with someone on the first date. Actually I felt like I knew him pretty well. In bed he was the answer to a maiden's prayer. I don't even want to think about where he learned to do all of the things he knew how to do. The next night he invited me over to his place for dinner. It meant breaking another date with Harry, but I didn't care. Ken sent out for Chinese, and we ate by candlelight. During the night on the way to the bathroom I looked out his bedroom window at mine across the way. My cat was sitting on the sill staring out and wondering where the hell I was.

Two weeks later we wrapped Cass Timberlaine. She didn't have another picture scheduled, and everybody assumed she'd use the time to plan her wedding. The columnists had been having a field day. I thought they would announce their engagement at the wrap party, but they didn't. I had been seeing Ken practically every night since we met, and I was as much in love as she was. After I said I was busy four times in a row Harry finally came right out and asked me what was going on.

"I've changed."

"Wadda ya mean?"

"I mean I think we should cool it."

"Is there another guy?"

"Yeah."

"Are you going to marry him?"

"Yes."

Harry isn't exactly Cesar Romero in the smooth manners department, but his heart's in the right place, and he wished me all the best. Hortense, whose brother Mort went to high school with him told me Harry was pretty shook up. I was sorry, but, as I said to Hortense, what am I supposed to do about it? To tell the truth Ken hadn't mentioned marriage yet. Of course it had only been three weeks since we started seeing each other, and men take longer than women about some things. I decided to use my time off between pictures to look for a bigger apartment. Neither Ken's place nor mine was big enough for two. For the next month things went along mostly fine. Ken was working on a detective picture, he had more than two lines for a change, and I was being domestic, cooking occasionally and planning the future. I took up horseback riding and tennis both of which Ken was good at. And I continued to look at apartments.

I said, mostly fine, because there was a fly in the ointment, maybe a couple of flies. For one thing Ken would announce out of the blue that he was going to be busy without telling me what he was going to be busy at. After five nights of bliss in his bed, I'd find myself back where I started, staring out my window at his, waiting for his light to come on. For another thing when I'd ask him to look at an apartment I liked he'd be noncommittal when I asked him what he thought. Hortense told me to come right out and ask him what his intentions were, but I couldn't. Men hate being cornered like that. The previous week Ty Power took a swing at a reporter who pestered him trying to find out if they were going to get married. I had been wondering what was going on with those two. Then I got the invitation to the party.

It was so like her, pink, with two hearts entwined. She was throwing it in his honor, and it was RSVP no less. I thought it was a beautiful way to announce an engagement. I shopped for days and finally decided on a changeable taffeta in turquoise with a full, three-quarter length skirt and a tight bodice. Ken didn't own a white dinner jacket, so I bought him one and left it on his doorstep where he'd find it when he came home from the studio that night. As soon as I heard his car door slam I went into my bedroom to look out the window. He was wearing the jacket when he switched on his bedroom light. He must have stood in front of the mirror for half and hour modeling it. God, he was gorgeous.

I'm really glad I was invited to that party, because everyone else in Hollywood was. The cars were backed up on Roxbury Drive all the way to Santa Monica Boulevard. When you finally reached her house there were attendants to park your car for you. It was some affair let me tell you. Everywhere you looked you saw a famous face. I could tell Ken was impressed. She and Ty greeted the guests out by the pool under a canopy of flowers. She was radiant, in pink of course, but his smile seemed forced, and he looked like he needed a shave. When I introduced Ken to her she raked him with her eyes, and when she kissed me she asked into my ear where I got him. We sat with the Metro crowd. She'd invited the crew from the Cass Timberlaine shoot, so it was like a reunion. Ken kept disappearing. He said he was working the room. I was surprised to see him on the dance floor with her. When I mentioned it to him on the way home he told me she'd asked him.

The big surprise of the evening though was that there was no engagement announcement. I mean the theme of the party was love and the entwined hearts on the invitations were repeated on the napkins, stamped on the butter pats, and carved out in a huge ice sculpture on the buffet table. Hortense was on the phone bright and early the next morning to hear all about it. She told me that Louella, according to what she wrote in her column that morning, was as surprised as everyone else. I looked out my bedroom window while I talked to Hortense. Ken's bed was unmade, the royal blue bedspread bunched up at its foot. He hadn't been in the mood when we came home from the party, and I slept in my own bed. The turquoise taffeta hung on my closet door. There was a large stain on the skirt where I'd dropped a raw oyster.

The next week Louella broke the news. Ty had taken off for a two month tour of Europe and Africa, alone. She, according to Louella, was planning to spend some time in New York. I folded the newspaper and wondered what it all meant. While I was getting a can of cat food out of the kitchen cabinet I saw the Bullocks Wilshire truck backing out of the driveway between my place and Ken's. There were two large boxes left on his doorstep. Things weren't right between us either. We hadn't spent any time together since the party. His picture had wrapped, and he had been away most of the time since, sleeping at his place only one night in the past five. I was beside myself, but I was trying to keep a grip on it.

All that afternoon I kept looking out the window at those boxes on his doorstep. He didn't get home until after dark. By that time I was sitting in my bedroom with the lights off, waiting. The cat was asleep on my bed having given up trying to get me away from the window to feed her. Now, I watched Ken pick up the boxes and carry them inside. He must have been opening them in the living room, because the bedroom light didn't go on right away. When it did he was holding two suitcases, nice leather ones. He put the bigger one on the bed and stepped back to admire it. I watched him toy with the lock and slowly run his fingers back and forth over the leather. He leaned over and sniffed it. Then he started packing. She was always extravagant when it came to presents. She gave me a diamond pin for Christmas.

The next day I signed a lease for a place in Beachwood Canyon. Two weeks later, moving day, Hortense called to find out if I had seen the papers. I had. They were full of the news about her new romance with Dan Topping, a man from New York. I wondered when Ken would be back. The night he left, while he was packing, he tried to call me several times. I watched him dial the telephone next to his bed. The ringing woke up the cat, and she started meowing right away for her supper. I went to the kitchen and felt around in the dark for the can of cat food I'd left on the counter when I got distracted earlier that afternoon. I managed to get the can open and the food into the cat dish without turning on a light. The phone rang a couple of times after I got into bed, and then his lights went out, and then it didn't ring anymore.

He didn't get back before I moved, thank God. drove by his apartment recently. His car was parked in the front, the top down. Hortense says I should have answered the phone that night just to hear what he had to say. What difference does it make what he had to say? Hortense and I don't think alike. The studio still doesn't have a picture lined up for her, so I'm using the time to take a shorthand course. You never know. Apparently she's going to marry the New York guy and spend some time living on the east coast. I love my new place. There's a swimming pool for the tenants, and from my bedroom window you can see the Hollywood Sign.

JUST THE WAY I AM

Joshua was washing dishes when he heard the commercial on the TV in the living room. It was selling tires and the dialog, spoken by an actor playing a race car driver, was delivered with an Italian accent. He hurried into the living room where his roommate Ray stood in front of the screen in his undershorts flossing his teeth.

"Didn't you audition for that?" asked Ray.

"I knew you say that."

"I can see why you didn't get it."

"What do you mean?"

"Well, look at that guy," he called from his bedroom, "they were obviously looking for someone more rugged than you are."

"You're so goddamn tactful. You should be a diplomat instead of a piano player in a cocktail lounge."

Ray came back into the living room wearing trousers now and carrying his shoes and socks. "I'm not a piano player in a cocktail lounge. I'm a musical director for major Hollywood productions currently between gigs. My work at the Blue Grotto offers me opportunities to meet women and, incidentally, to pay the rent."

"Melrose Avenue chicky booms with green spiked hair."

"You're turning into an old fart," said Ray

After he left Joshua decided to take a shower before Lila came over to practice a scene they were working on for the scene study class they took together. The scene was from Born Yesterday, and they thought they had it down until their teacher, a former RKO contract player whose career peaked in the Forties, stopped them after the first few lines.

"Go back and do your homework," she said. "That dialog is fluff, and you have to play fluff with your feet solidly on the ground. You two look like understudies in a road company of Waiting For Godot."

Stunned, they return to their seats. "I'm scared of that bitch," said Lila during the break. "I don't think she likes me."

"Better her than a critic from the Times," said Joshua.

In the shower he thought about Lila. He wasn't sure about her as an actress, but he liked her as a person. As a matter of fact he wanted to take her to bed, but he hadn't figured out how she felt about him. Preternaturally neat, a quality he liked in women, she was totally dedicated to her career. Every day she forced her self to do five things to promote it. A picture sent to a casting agent counted as one thing as did acting class. An audition counted for two things, and if she worked she gave herself credit for five. Joshua admired and envied her dedication. He tended to rely on serendipity. Last week on his way to the dentist in Westwood he rode up on the elevator with Clint Eastwood. Before he could initiate any conversation, however, Eastwood got off. That's the way it happens he thought as he watched the elevator door close leaving him alone. You meet the people you're supposed to meet when you're supposed to meet them. He heard a knock on the door just as he finished dressing. "Come in," he called from the bedroom, "it's open."

She was folding her sweater when he joined her in the living room. "Are you Jewish?" she asked.

"No."

"Is Ray?"

"No."

"Why to you have a mezuzah on the doorframe?"

"The people who lived here before must have put it there. Someone painted around it, and if we take it off it'll leave a bare spot. Besides, we need all the help we can get. Hello."

"Hi."

"Do you want anything, soda, coffee, juice, tea, me?"

"What?"

"Coffee, tea, or me. A flight attendant once wrote a book with that title."

"Flight attendants, now that's a group. Do you have any diet soda?"

They ran through the scene a couple of times. Then they tried it with Joshua saying Lila's lines and her saying his. Next they sang the lines to each other, and then they did it again, substituting la la la for the syllables of the words.

"I wish I knew more about what she wants us to do with this," said Lila. "Let's face it, a lot of it sounds like sitcom."

"How do you feel about this woman, do you like her?"

"I never get emotionally involved with the characters I play."

"I do," said Joshua. "Did you eat?"

"Not for a while. I could do a sandwich."

They walked over to Fairfax Avenue stopping to browse at the newsstand on the corner. Lila picked up a copy of the weekly newspaper for actors that listed casting calls. While she flipped through it Joshua scanned the covers of the skin magazines displayed near the cash register. One pictured a model who resembled his seventh grade teacher. He resisted the urge to take it from the rack for a closer look. The old man who owned the newsstand could be hard on the casual voyeur.

"In the library you can read for free," Joshua once heard him say to a distinguished looking older man who was pouring over a glossy shot of what looked like at least twenty women cavorting in a hot tub. "Me, I gotta make a living." Mortified and so rattled that he couldn't replace the magazine in its holder the man forced it, tearing the cover. He hurried away.

The old man called after him, "*Shmuck*."

Lila paid for the newspaper she had been looking at. "I never got a paying job through this thing," she said to Joshua.

"Hey lady," said the old man, "for guarantees you go to Costco."

Lila took her change. "Everybody's a comedian in this town."

In the deli they ordered corn beef sandwiches and celery tonic.

"So how's your life?" asked Joshua.

"Funny you should ask. I had an experience today that caused me to seriously question my whole commitment to the profession."

"My god, what happened?"

"You know Gregory? That guy in class with the nose job?"

"The one who always does monologs with a British accent?"

"No, that's Stanley. Gregory is the one who always wears tank tops with plunging arm holes."

"How do you know he has a nose job?"

"Because I have eyes to see. Anyway, he tells me that his cousin is a casting agent and offers to get my headshot to him which he does. Today I met the cousin."

"And?"

"He has an office in Century City." She took a sip of celery tonic. "I'd like a straw if we can get the waitress's eye. Oh never mind I'll get it." She started to get out of the booth.

"I'll get it," said Joshua sliding out. "Sit."

The waitress had brought the sandwiches by the time he came back with the straw.

"Do you want anything besides mustard?" asked Lila.

"No."

"Good, because that's all she brought."

"You were saying?"

"I figured if he's successful enough to have an office in Century City he's obviously on the up and up."

"You never make assumptions like that in Hollywood."

"Would you mind? You're ruining my flow."

"Sorry."

"Anyway, we're having a nice meeting. He seemed very interested in the showcase I'm doing in Van Nuys next month."

"I thought you dropped out of that."

"I did, but I heard Richard Dreyfus is going to be there, so I got back in."

"They always start rumors like that. I once did one where they told us Robert Altman was in the audience. It turned out to be a guy with a beard who looked like him."

"Anyway, all of a sudden this guy comes out with, so how do you feel about nudity?"

"Oh, shit."

"Have you ever had an experience where your whole life flashes before your eyes? I mean, I didn't just get off the artichoke truck, but I was nonplused to say the least."

"What did you do?"

"I showed him my tits."

"What did he do?"

"He looked at them."

"Did he say anything?"

"I really think I surprised the horny bastard. He kept saying, very nice, very nice. I mean, picture the scene. We're on the eighteenth floor overlooking the whole Los Angles Basin, there was no smog today if you'll remember, and I'm sitting there with my boobs out across the desk from this pathetic lecher in Gucci loafers who keeps saying, very nice, very nice. Talk about existential moments."

"I guess it's all in a day's work. Do you think you'll get a job out of it?"

"There's probably one chance in ten thousand."

"Are you going to tell Gregory?

"No."

Later, walking to her car Joshua asked her if she wanted to run through it one more time.

"No," she said. "I'm tired. Let's do it once more

on Saturday morning before class."

Walking in the quiet dark, the scent of orange blossoms in the balmy night air got to him, and he took her hand. When they got to her car he waited for her to unlock the door before he opened his arms. She stepped right into them and made herself comfortable, and he found her lips with no trouble at all. She even put a promise into his mouth with her tongue. After he watched her drive off he decided to walk over to Melrose and have a beer at the Blue Grotto.

Ray was spotlighted at the piano playing Cottage For Sale when Joshua walked into the lounge. Seated at a small table close to the piano was a platinum blond woman in a silver lame dress looking at Ray with rapt attention. He was striving for nonchalance as he took the melody farther out and subtly started to work in the theme from Exodus. When they recognized what he was doing a foursome seated in a banquette applauded politely. Ray didn't acknowledge the applause, but Joshua could see his nostrils flare. Joshua sat down at the bar next to two young women and ordered a beer.

"Don't mention stinger to me," said one of the women, a redhead, to her companion. "I had two of them at Yvonne's shower and barfed all over the baby blanket Sharon gave her."

"Let's have gin and tonic, then," said the other one. Her hair was brown and cut very short. She wore hoop earrings.

The redhead looked at the mirrored wall behind the bar and saw Joshua smiling. "You must think I'm awful," she said.

"No."

"Well I want you to know I replaced the blanket."

He nodded. "My name is Josh."

"I'm Lorna," she said, "and this is my friend Michelle."

Michelle smiled.

"Please to meet you. Do you live in LA?"

"Glendale," said Lorna.

"What do you do?" he asked.

"I work in a doctor's office and Michelle is in marketing."

"I sell make-up," said Michelle, "in Bullocks. What do you do?"

"I'm an actor."

She lit up. "Oh wow. Have I seen you in anything?"

"I had a telephone company commercial running last year during the holidays, but I was wearing a robot outfit so you wouldn't have recognized me."

"I think I saw it."

"Right now," he lied, "I'm up for a part on The Young and the Restless." The truth was that he had learned that afternoon the he didn't get the part.

"The Young and the Restless," she said, "I watched that all during high school. What a coincidence."

"Do you know anyone famous?" asked Lorna.

"I have a nodding acquaintance with Clint Eastwood."

"Oh my god, Clint Eastwood," said Michelle. "What's he like?"

"He's quiet."

Ray announced that he was taking a break and joined them. Joshua made the introductions.

"Did you notice that blonde sitting by the piano?" asked Ray.

"What's not to notice?" said Lorna. "There's something about the way the spotlight reflects off the lame."

"She was Lana Turner's stand-in," said Ray.

"I don't believe this," said Michelle. "I just watched The Postman Always Rings Twice two nights ago."

"She knows people in the music department at Disney," said Ray, "and on Saturday night she's stopping by again with a few of them."

"Are you an actor, too?" asked Lorna.

"You're pulling my leg," said Ray. "Do I look like an actor?"

"You could be."

Ray's nostrils flared again. "I have to get back to work. What do you want to hear?"

"Just the Way You Are" said Lorna.

"You have got to be kidding," said Michelle. "You took the words right out of my mouth."

Ray excused himself and headed for the men's room. When he came out he took his seat at the piano and played the request. By the time he had finished, Lorna and Michelle were talking to a couple of men seated at their other side. Joshua finished his beer and bid the women goodnight. Ray had launched into "She's Funny That Way" and was singing it to the blonde in the silver lame.

Joshua walked along Melrose Avenue and for the first time since he'd gotten the news that afternoon thought about his rejection by the casting people from The Young and the Restless. Rejection seared him no matter how hard he tried to steel himself. Every time it happened his self-esteem was violated, his dreams were mocked, and all that he took himself to be was threatened by pessimism and despair. He knew that he had talent, but a lot of people in Hollywood did. The question was did he have perseverance.

When he got home he opened the freezer section of the refrigerator. There was nothing but some spaghetti sauce and a pint of gourmet chocolate ice cream with a note in Ray's handwriting attached with a rubber band.

"Do not," it read, "repeat NOT, eat this ice cream."

Leaving the note and the rubber band in the freezer he took the ice cream carton into the living room and ate from it while he watched the news. had had enough he switched off the TV and returned the carton to the freezer replacing Ray's note with the rubber band. Later, in his bedroom undressing for bed he looked at his naked body in the dresser mirror. He had good shoulders, his stomach was flat, his legs were straight, and everything was in proportion. He imagined himself in a casting office standing naked like that, brazen yet modest, proud yet vulnerable, dignified yet lickerish. Very nice, the casting people would say, very nice.

REJOICE

Passively, like a bored viewer watching a television screen with the sound turned low, Brodsky stared up at the woman, as she tried to get through to him. She was old but not as old as he. She had put her shopping bag, soup greens and a *challah* sticking out of its top, on the steps of the synagogue in front of which he'd fallen. Leaning over him so that her face was close to his she held his eyes with hers as she spoke. He couldn't make out most of the words, but the look on her face told him she resented this forced interruption to what he guessed were her pre-Sabbath errands. His eyeglasses, hearing aid attached, lay on the sidewalk near his head, but he made no effort to reach for them. At his age you took your pleasure where you found it, and for the present he was content to lie there in the sun, the warmth from the sidewalk cement seeping into his bones. As far as he could tell nothing had gotten broken when he fell. He wiggled his fingers and toes. He moved his head from side to side. The woman must have inferred that he was responding negatively to something she said, because she stood up abruptly and scanned Beverly Boulevard for assistance. Spying an approaching *Chassid* she pounced upon him and dragged him toward the supine Brodsky who by now had retrieved his eyeglasses. By the time they reached himhe had put them on, hearing aid in place. "Help me up, please," he said to the *Chassid*, a young man whose shiny black beard matched the fabric in the long coat he wore.

The man reached down to take Brodsky's arm. "Where do you live?" he asked

"The Sunny View, right around the corner."

"I'll take you there."

"I'm going, then," said the woman. She picked up her shopping bag and hurried off. "Good *Shabbes*," she called over her shoulder.

Brodsky called after her, "Thanks for your help." If she heard him she didn't acknowledge it. The *Chassid* helped him to his feet, and they headed for The Sunny View Retirement Haven where Brodsky had a room. "Brodsky," he said to the man.

"What?"

"Brodsky, my name is Avram Brodsky."

The man didn't respond. He thinks I'm *treyf*, thought Brodsky, because I'm wearing walking shorts and sandals. The temperature was in the seventies, but the *Chassid*, in addition to the long black coat, was wearing a black wool suit and a broad brimmed hat trimmed in fur. He was obviously on his way to services. Brodsky didn't understand the *Chassidic* Jews. He had lived among them all his life, but he had never been able to establish anything but the most superficial relationship with any of them. His parents had been liberal thinkers, Socialists, and he had been reared to respect all religious belief while keeping it at a distance. The orthodoxy of the *Chassidim* with its intolerance of liberalism, however, he found repulsive. "They're backward," he said to his best friend, Peschel. "They keep their wives pregnant and in the kitchen, and they take no interest in the world outside their little corner."

"As my father, may he rest in peace, used to say, live and let live," said Peschel.

It was dinner hour at The Sunny View, so Brodsky and the *Chassid* didn't have to run the gauntlet through the nosey group usually soaking up sun on the terrace. Broksky thanked God for small favors. "You can leave me here," he said to the Chassid when they reached the front door. He offered his hand. The man let go of Brodsky's arm and walked away without acknowledging it. Well fuck you Mr. Fashion Plate, thought Brodsky. Go pray to that god of yours who expects you to dress like that. The landlady's fat grandson, Marshall, was seated behind the desk when Brodsky entered the front hall. Marshall, whose mother had run off with a Hell's Angel when he was five, was now nineteen and a desultory student in junior college. Brodsky knew he was an unhappy boy, and he tried to be kind, but it was difficult. The kid was an obnoxious little shit. Marshall put down the magazine he was reading. "What happened to your nose?"

He must have scraped it when he fell. "I tried putting it where it didn't belong."

"You fell down again, didn't you? That's the second time in a month. One of these days you're going to kill yourself. You need to get a walker."

"And one of these days you're going to make contact with your brain."

"You missed dinner. Brisket. You can probably get dessert if you hurry."

"Forget it. I'm not hungry." He lied. He was hungry, but he would have to pay for a seat in the dining room by answering questions about his bruised nose, and that would lead to a discussion about the pros and cons of exercise, and finally, there would be pronouncements, delivered second hand, made by sons and nephews who were doctors.

Today was Brodsky's wedding anniversary, and he needed to be alone, so he climbed the stairs to his second floor room. Of the twelve residents at The Sunny View he had the best room, in the front, with a private bath. He paid more, but he could afford it. With a pension from his union and Social Security he was doing better than most. He had come out here during the Great Depression to get away from the cold in the East, and he found work as a dishwasher in the commissary at Metro Goldwyn Mayer Studios. Before he retired thirty-five years later he had risen to the position of full chef in charge of salads, but during the *tsuris* of 1947 he was accused, correctly, of supporting several organizations that turned out to be, unknown to him, infiltrated by Communists. Brodsky was never a Communist, but a witch hunt was going on, and when you're accused at a time like that you're tainted, guilty or not.

He was luckier than most of them. He didn't lose his job, but he was no longer in charge of salads, and he spent the remainder of his years in the commissary behind the pie counter. Peschel urged him to leave the studio and join him selling hospital supplies, but Brodsky was no salesman, and he knew it. Besides, he told Peschel, he could never quit show business. Brodsky's wife, Sylvie, had often told him he was capable of anything, but frankly he wasn't that ambitious. The oldest of five children, he had started working when he was eight years old getting up every morning at dawn seven days a week to sell newspapers on the streets of New York. By the time he was thirteen he was working as a presser in his father's tailor shop.

Brodsky had to quit school, but the others made it through thanks to him. They never forgot the help he gave them, and over the years the gratitude checks came from the East enabling him and Sylvie, there were no children, to buy a bungalow on Spaulding. Now all of them were gone, may they rest in peace, except his sister Esther who sent a card every year at Rosh Hashanah from a retirement home in Lakewood, New Jersey.

In his room he opened the closet door and took down from the shelf a box of pictures that he and Sylvie had acquired over the years. They were always going to put them into an album some rainy afternoon, but in California there are so few rainy afternoons, and eventually there were too many pictures, and then Sylvie was gone. Brodsky sat in the Morris chair by the window with the box in his lap. He poured himself a glass of peppermint schnapps and started to go through the pictures. He had done this, with the pictures and a schnapps or two, for the past six anniversaries since Sylvie died. It had become his ritual, and he had been thinking about it when he fell. His life was in that box, his parents with him and his brothers and sisters at Coney Island on the Fourth of July, their one and only outing every year, his baby brother Izzie on the day of his *Bar Mitzvah*, Esther and her husband in front of their house in Teaneck, his brother Mort pointing to his shingle the day he opened his dental practice, it was all there. Most of the pictures, however, were of Sylvie and him and Peschel. The three musketeers they called themselves.

Abe Brodsky and Leon Peschel had been friends since they were boys together on the Lower East Side. Brodsky couldn't remember a time in his life when Peschel wasn't in it. When the time came to leave New York and strike out for California they did it together. Getting off the train in the blinding sunlight they went together to Woolworths to buy dark glasses. Together they took a room in a boarding house on Curson, and when Sylvia Lapin the landlord's comely daughter captured Brodsky's heart, Peschel's was similarly ensnared. Sylvie liked them both, and for the first year, before things got serious, she had two suitors. On Sundays they would go to Santa Monica on the trolley, walking the pier, riding the carrousel. Sometimes Peschel and Sylvie would go in swimming while Brodsky who hated salt water would sit on a blanket in the sand and watch them. Finally Brodsky, deeply in love, proposed. Sylvie hesitated. She had been expecting a proposal, but she thought she was going to have more time. Brodsky was taken aback by her hesitation, but before he could remark on it she said yes. Then she asked him to let her tell Peschel. That night lying in his bed across from Peschel's Brodsky listened to his roommate's snores and realized that one of them had to be hurt. He thanked God it wasn't him.

For their honeymoon the Brodskys went to San Francisco, and after three days Peschel, who was on the road at the time selling typewriters, met them there. During the day they walked the hilly streets laughing and joking the way they always did. At night they dined on the wharf or in Chinatown. Afterwards they would take in a show. It was only when they said goodnight in the hotel lobby, when the Brodskys went to their room and Peschel went to his, that there was between the two men a momentary awkwardness. If Sylvie noticed it she never let on. Peschel never married. He ate often at the Brodskys, always on Friday night and for all the holidays. They took their vacations together. The fact that no children came along bound them closer together as a family, Peschel filling a place at the table that might have served as a reminder to Abe and Sylvie of their childlessness. When Sylvie died, quickly thank God, of a massive stroke, Peschel was there for Brodsky to lean on. There were days when all Brodsky wanted to do was to die too, to lie next to her in the ground away from the suffocating loneliness. It was Peschel who took his friend to the steam baths, to Las Vegas, once even to New York where they walked all over the Lower East Side and marveled at how it had all changed.

Relaxed now from the schnapps Brodsky continued to flip slowly through the faded snapshots. Suddenly he stopped. He was holding one he hadn't noticed before, or, if he had, he didn't remember it now. It showed Sylvie in a polka dot dress she'd had made for the wedding of a man Brodsky worked with at the studio. When they were courting the Brodsky's song had been Polka Dots and Moonbeams, and at the reception he asked the band to play it. While they danced Sylvie sang in his ear and caressed the back of his neck with her finger tips. In the picture Brodsky was holding now Sylvie was standing in front of the Hollywood Roosevelt Hotel. It was a profile shot, because she was smiling into the face of the man standing next to her who returned the smile. It was Peschel. Brodsky poured himself another schnapps and drank it while he continued to look at the picture. When he finished the drink he dropped the picture into the box, replaced the cover and put the box back on the closet shelf. He sat down on his bed, picked up the telephone on the bedside table and keyed in a number. Peschel answered.

"Great minds work on the same frequency," he said "I was just going to call you."

"Do you want to eat Chinese tomorrow night?" asked Brodsky.

"Sounds good, where?"

"Why do you always ask where when I suggest Chinese? We've been going to the Mandarin Garden for fifteen years, and you ask where?"

"It's polite, and my mother, may she rest in peace, taught me to be polite."

"Is six o'clock alright?"

"Six it is."

"See you then. Goodnight."

"Goodnight, Abe."

The next morning Brodsky slept in. The schnapps had dehydrated him and during the night he kept waking up with a dry mouth. He had to keep refilling the water glass by his bed. While he was up he would urinate. His bladder had become a problem. His prostate gland was enlarged, perfectly normal for a man his age according to his doctor. "It's squeezing your urinary tract," said the doctor. "Nothing to worry about." Standing in front of the bowl in the quiet nights, Brodsky wished the doctor hadn't told him that. Now when he got up to piss he always pictured his prostate gland blown up like a balloon inside him, and he would remember when he could sleep right through. He went down to lunch at noon and then spent the afternoon reading. He tried to watch the news, but all of it irritated him, and he switched it off. Later, on the way to the Mandarin Garden the cab driver, newly arrived in this country from God knows where, got lost and had to keep asking Brodsky for directions. Brodsky tried to be patient, but it was an effort, and he resented having to make it. Peschel was seated in a booth when Brodsky arrived.

"We missed the early bird special by half an hour," he said.

"Screw the early bird special. When I want lunch I'll go out to lunch."

"So stop the universe and I'll get out of it. I was only making conversation. Have a drink, you look like you could use one."

"What's the matter with the way I look?"

"Nothing. I was referring to your ass which obviously has a hair across it."

Brodsky ordered a glass of seltzer. "What have you been up to?"

"I'm changing my will," said Peschel.

"You're cutting me out?"

"Of course I'm not cutting you out, but you're not going to be around forever. Who knows? You could go before I do. It's when you're gone. I want everything left to the Community Center instead of to my worthless nephew who doesn't know he has an uncle except when he needs something."

Brodsky studied the menu. "Do what you want to do. Let's eat. I'm hungry."

They ordered pot stickers, lemon chicken and spicy shrimp in black bean sauce.

"But not too spicy," said Peschel to the waiter.

Brodsky snapped the menu shut. "To hell with the shrimp. Order something else."

"Now what's wrong? All I said was not too spicy."

"That's like ordering a chocolate sundae without the chocolate sauce. Can't you for once in your life be a little adventurous?"

"Can't we get the hot sauce on the side?"

"It's not the same. Every time we come here we have this discussion."

"And I always give in."

"So give," said Brodsky.

Peschel nodded at the waiter. "Bring the shrimp."

"You want a chocolate sundae, too?" asked the waiter.

"No, Groucho," said Brodsky.

They ate the meal in silence. Peschel made several attempts at conversation, but Brodsky replied in monosyllables. When they finished the waiter cleared the table and brought fortune cookies.

Peschel read his. "You need not worry about your future. What did you get?"

"You are blessed in your friends," read Brodsky. "What a laugh."

"What are you talking about?"

"I'm talking about you fucked my wife, you son of a bitch."

The teacup Peschel was bringing to his mouth stopped on the way and stayed there in midair, six inches from its destination. Then, returning it to the table he stared at it, his hand still encircling it.

"Explain."

"Explain what? You're the one who's got the explaining to do."

"Explain why you're accusing me after all these years."

"Because I've never in my life set foot in the Hollywood Roosevelt Hotel, and I have reason to know that you've been there with my wife. In fact, I have proof."

"There can be no proof of what never happened. You're getting excited about a fictional event. I never did that with your wife in the Roosevelt. Relax."

"Oh, thank God." Brodsky slumped back in his seat. "What a relief."

"This is not to say we never did it anywhere else," said Peschel.

"Do you have any nitroglycerine with you?"

Peschel took a small bottle from his shirt pocket and pushed it across the table. "It happened the night she told me she was going to marry you. Of course I had suspected it. She loved us both, sure, but she leaned toward you. That was clear to me."

Brodsky placed a pill under his tongue. "How could you betray me like that?"

"I didn't quite see it like that. I saw myself as the one who was betrayed. Everything had been so wonderful, the three of us, the good times, and now it was all over. Now it was you and Sylvie with Leon looking in."

"You could have found a wife. We could have all been as close as ever."

"If you'll remember we were as close as ever. And you're forgetting something."

"What?"

"That I loved Sylvie as much as you did, and I stayed in love with her right up to the end, just like you did. Except for a couple of adventures on the road I never looked at another woman. Having known Sylvie like that, if only once, I was able to forgive you both and continue our lives. She seemed to understand everything even though we never discussed it again. And hey, it worked out, didn't it?"

"I don't know."

"Did you ever doubt her love for you?"

"No."

"Let's face it I made more money that you did. Did she ever make you think she'd rather be with me than with you?"

"No."

"I call that working out."

"You're right. It worked out."

They drank their tea in silence, and when they finished Peschel signaled for the check.

"I'll get it," said Brodsky.

"You got it last time."

"I want to."

"OK, thanks."

Brodsky felt drained as they waited for a cab in front of the restaurant. Light-headedness had replaced his anger. He wondered if he was having a stroke, but he decided it too pleasant a sensation for anything as serious as that. It was more like euphoria.

"You couldn't put his in a story," he said to Peschel. "Nobody would believe it."

"So what if nobody would believe it? It was our lives. Only we have to believe it. My father, may he rest in peace, used to say, don't judge and don't compare."

Two cabs pulled up to the curb. Brodsky

opened the door of the first one and turned to Peschel. "Just tell me one thing. Where did you do it?"

"That isn't any of your business. Goodnight, Abe."

Brodsky hugged him. "Goodnight, Leon."

The feeling of well being continued in the cab as Brodsky made his way home. He wasn't ready for his room yet, he needed to be outdoors under the stars, so he told the driver to let him out a couple of blocks from The Sunny View. He decided to walk by the house he and Sylvie had owned and lived in for so many years. In the moonlight he saw a dog dish on the top step to the porch and a tipped over tricycle in the small front yard. There was a light on in the living room, but he couldn't see any sign of people through the slats of the blind. Venetian blinds. How Sylvie had hated them. What would she say to see them hanging in her windows? Once again a wave of well being washed over him, and he smiled. He couldn't be more aware of Sylvie if she had been standing there next to him in the dark, her scent invading his nostrils. None of it matters, he thought, it's all a dream. Still smiling, he headed for The Sunny View. He checked his box in the front hall for mail.

"There's nothing for you," Marshall announced from behind the desk. He had a book in front of him. He must have been studying for a change.

"So I see." Brodsky was determined to be

pleasant. "What are you studying?"

"Television production. It's my major."

Brodsky tried to summon an affable reply, but nothing came. Television, he thought as he climbed the stairs to his room, the whole world is turning into a giant computer and this *shlemiel* majors in television. Then he thought of Peschel's father, don't judge, don't compare, and he tried to picture Marshall as President of CBS. In his room, he decided to have a bath. He usually took showers, but he was still sore from yesterday's fall, and a soak would feel good. When the tub was half full he moved to turn off the water, mindful of the Governor's pleas to go easy. Normally Brodsky considered it his civic duty to conserve water. "There's only tonight," he said out loud as he let the water run, "and it's no more than I deserve."

After his bath he put on clean pajamas and turned down the bed. He went to the window to open it wider for the night. The man in the house next door, into whose living room Brodsky could see, was watching a pornographic movie on a television screen no more than twenty feet away. Brodsky retrieved his glasses from the nightstand, adjusted the hearing aid, and turned out the light. He kneeled down to watch, elbows resting on the windowsill. He couldn't make out all the details, but he could see enough to hold his interest. A naked man was lying spread-eagled on a bed while three equally naked women were all over him doing things that Brodsky had never experienced personally. He watched, kneeling like that, until he started getting shooting pains in his legs and up into his lower back. He thought of moving his chair over to the window but decided he'd had enough and stood up to go to bed. It was then that he realized he was hard, not just semi-tumescent, to use a phrase from a book on sex and aging that he'd read recently, but hard. He hurried to his bed. Moving his hand slowly on his erection he thought of how it never gets boring, that wonderful tickling in the groin. Then he closed his eyes while images of MGM's beauties from days gone by rolled across the screen behind his eyelids Lana Turner licking meringue from her top lip the day he gave her a sample taste Nina Foch pointing to the peach cobbler her skin like porcelain in the florescent light Esther Williams winking at him when he put an extra dollop of whipped cream on her cherry pie her hair held rigid by Vaseline her body supple under a terry cloth robe. Then he thought of Sylvie and Peschel doing it. He stopped, censored. But it was too late for stopping. It's ok, he thought, moving his hand faster, I love you Sylvie Leon it's ok Leon Sylvie Sylvie love what love love love love love ...love....love...

L.A. ANGEL

Bobby Spinelli never even wanted to be a singer. He always maintained that it had been forced upon him. In college, one of his girlfriends who was kind of spacey said that his voice was a gift from the universe. Growing up in show business, his old man built sets at Warner Brothers, Bobby was under no illusions about what it takes to make it. Gift from the universe or not, what he had was a pleasant baritone, no more, no less. That, he calculated, was not enough to take him to where he wanted to go, the place left vacant by his idol James Dean. As soon as he picked up his Associate Degree in theater arts from Santa Monica City College he would head for New York to make a name for himself on the stage. He had a handsome face, a lithe California body, and a compelling need to show them off. He planned to go with these and to forget about the baritone.

The singing thing got started when he was in the seventh grade, and Sister Pauline cast him as Prince Charming in a musical version of Cinderella that she wrote. He was reluctant, it seemed vaguely sissified, but his parents decided for him. "You don't argue with the nuns," said his father. Prince Charming might have been the end of it, but in High School sex came into his life, and he learned to use his voice to attract girls. Dancing close, he would nibble pliant earlobes and insinuate his songs. The girls couldn't get enough. Later, when he was in college, a friend of his father's at the studio got him a job as a backup singer. It was boring work, he almost hated it, but it was better than waiting tables, and at night he dreamed about Schubert Alley and neon lights.

A month before graduation and his departure for New York he was asked by the studio to dub the singing voice of a hot new actor who couldn't carry a tune. The same week Bobby recorded the song the actor was busted for propositioning an undercover cop in Griffith Park, and the studio yanked the film. Bobby thought that was the end of it until one of the sound engineers sent the tape over to a friend in the record division. The friend smelled a hit and talked his people into releasing it as a single. The song, L.A. Angel, was written by a paraplegic ex-Green Beret. It was about a soldier who exchanges waves with a woman standing on the dock as his troopship pulls out of Long Beach on its way to war.

The soldier, carrying the memory of the woman, is blinded in battle. The last chorus finds him lying in a hospital bed with the woman's image having become a symbol of everything he fought for. He vows to love her until he dies. It wasn't exactly God Bless America, and initial sales were just so so. Then John Wayne mentioned it one night on Carson. The next day L.A. Angel took off like a big-ass bird. By the following week it was at the top of every chart that mattered.

Bobby hurriedly recorded nine more of the ex-Green Beret's songs for an album and went on a personal appearance tour. The record company had hopes that when the hit faded they could release another single and keep the ball rolling, but it didn't happen. The song stayed popular for almost a year, and the album went platinum, but Bobby never had another hit single. His agent had cut a bad deal on the first album, but he promised they'd make it up on the second one. The second one bombed, however, and Bobby's price went into the toilet. The following year he paid the rent with appearances at state fairs in the Midwest. After that he did a couple of years of dinner theater as Cornelius in Hello Dolly. When the local hayseed critics started making cracks about him being a little long in the tooth for the part that too dried up.

Back in Hollywood, he landed a part in a Roger Corman production that for some reason didn't get released. He tried a one-man show in a ninety-nine seat theater on Melrose Avenue, but that didn't work either. His savings lasted for two more years during which time he smoked a lot of weed and walked on the beach. When his rent check for the little pad in the Hills bounced he sobered up, got a cheaper place down on the flat lands between San Vicente and Doheny south of Sunset, and took a job driving a cab. By then he had been forgotten. Occasionally a passenger would say he looked familiar, but Bobby would deflect that by ignoring it and asking them what side of the street they wanted.

As for his hit record he played it occasionally, usually late at night. He'd come home from a ten-hour shift behind the wheel, have a shower, and then, lying on the sofa with a can of beer and a joint, he'd stare at the streetlight outside his living room window and wait for the drugs to kick in. He liked that time of day, the quiet deserted street outside, the neighboring windows mostly dark. The hot polluted air of the daytime city would have cooled by then, its sweetness artificially restored by the darkness. Lying there, his mind drifting like the balmy breeze that wafted through the open window, Bobby would hear the song in his mind, as if it were coming from a source far up in the hills. He knew of course he was imagining it, but he always marveled at how real it sounded. Sometimes he would play the album and think about James Dean. If the dope was good enough he would feel Dean's presence, as if the dead actor were sitting in the chair next to the sofa. He reveled in the company of his idol. Jimmy knew about lost opportunities, squandered talent, and careers that would never be. Bobby didn't have to explain to Jimmy. That spacey girl he knew in college would have called it cosmic, Jimmy brought down by a silver Porsche, Bobby done in by a song.

The ex-Green Beret hadn't fared too well either. Bobby saw him one day in front of Bullocks Westwood holding a sign that read, Nam Vet will work for food. He was filthy, and his face was wasted from booze.

Bobby had just dropped off a woman who had handed him her telephone number along with the fare. She'd interested him as soon as he picked her up in front of a high rise on Doheny near where he lived. Probably in her late thirties, she had a tight body and pretty face that had gone slightly hard the way faces do in this city. The scent of gardenia followed her into the cab. He was a sucker for gardenia.

"Go via Sunset," she said. "I have to stop at the optometrist."

Through the optometrist's window he watched her take a pair of glasses out of her bag and lay them on the counter. The optometrist nodded while he listened to her. When she got back in the cab she asked him if he minded if she smoked.

"Go ahead, I like it. I used to smoke myself."

"Did you manage to shake all your bad habits?"

"Just the expensive ones."

"The expensive ones are usually the most fun."

"I've still got a couple of cheap ones that are right up there."

She didn't reply. He looked at her in the rear view mirror. She was staring out the window while she smoked. She let him have a good look. She had nice features, good skin, and full lips. Hair, make-up,everything was top shelf. He pulled to a stop at the light in front of the Beverly Hills Hotel. The traffic on Sunset was moving right along for a change.

"I went to a party in that house," she said as

they drove by a sprawling low-slung ranch on a corner lot. "It wasn't A-list."

"More like an A minus?"

She laughed. "More like a B plus."

Gardenia perfume and a sexy laugh, he thought. I can't believe I'm getting turned on by a fare.

"Was it a good party?"

"It had its moments. Betty White was there."

"What was she like?"

"We didn't talk. Anyway, it turned into an orgy."

"Betty White at an orgy? Come on."

"She'd been gone for hours, but a lot of people stayed."

"I've been to parties like that."

"I'm sure you have." She didn't speak again until he turned down into Westwood Village. "Are you married?"

"No."

"Divorced?"

"No."

"Gay?"

"No."

He pulled up in front of the store. It was then that he noticed the guy who wrote L.A. Angel slouched in his wheelchair parked outside the revolving door. He's still wearing those fucking fatigues, thought Bobby.

"Are you going to take this?" She had opened the door and was leaning forward holding out the money along with a small light blue slip of paper. When he got home that night he posted it on his refrigerator door with a souvenir magnet from Universal Studios that some Japanese people had left in the cab. If he had a nickel for every time a sexy woman had palmed him a phone number during that year he was a record star he could be getting ready for retirement in Palm Springs. It was different now that he drove a cab. Most people ignored him or talked at him, wrapped in their own concerns or turned on by the sound of their own voices. He never married, settling instead for relationships with women whose circumstances tended to make the idea of marriage problematic. Bobby lived close to the surface of his skin, and marriage would have forced him to go deeper. He didn't want to do that. His last girlfriend, a dental hygienist, divorced, accused him of having a PeterPan complex. She had been acting strangely lately. He knew the signs.

"What the fuck is a Peter Pan complex?" They had just finished washing up after cooking hamburgers on the grill in her small Van Nuys back yard. Her seven year old son was watching a nature show in the living room.

"I've told you not to use that word in front of Adam."

"He didn't hear it. The TV's too loud."

"What's that supposed to mean?"

"What's what supposed to mean? You're not

making any sense."

"You don't relate to Adam. You never have."

"He's seven years old. He worships his father. I don't blame him for hating me. He thinks I'm going to take you away."

"Fat chance."

"Oh, God."

She switched off the kitchen light and went out the back door. "Peter Pan," she called back, "is a man locked into boyhood."

He followed her out to the patio and sat down next to her in the hammock. "Is Adam going to spend the night at Jackie's?"

"Yes."

"Is Bobby going to spend the night here?"

"If you want to. But you have to leave before Adam gets home tomorrow morning."

"Hey, I'm easy."

Adam came to the back door. "I'm leaving now, Mom," he said through the screen. "See you tomorrow."

"Is Jackie's mother here?"

"Yeah, out front. She said to hurry. She has to pick up Jackie's sister at the mall."

"Come kiss me."

Adam came outside wearing a back pack almost as big as he was.

"What are you carrying in that bag?" asked Bobby, "Your mattress?"

Adam ignored him and kissed his mother. "Can I go to the pool tomorrow?"

"We'll see. Say goodnight to Bobby."

He was already back in the kitchen when he mumbled goodnight.

After Adam left they sat for a while without talking. It was comfortable sitting together like that in the twilight. As a matter of fact, except for Adam, everything about her was comfortable. The kid next door was shooting baskets in the driveway until it got too dark for him to see.

She stood up. "I'm ready to turn in."

He followed her into the house. In the bedroom they got undressed without turning on a light. In bed she gave herself to him generously but without any passion. Afterwards, lying in the dark she turned on her side to face him. "This isn't working."

"Didn't you come?

"You know what I'm talking about."

Bobby knew. He'd had this conversation with other women over the years, and he saw no point in having it again. He got up and dressed in the dark. When he finished he knelt by the side of the bed and reached for her hand. He brought it to his lips.

"Have a good life," she said.

"You too."

"Make sure the door is locked."

He hadn't been seeing anyone else since then. He bowled every week with a bunch of guys from work, and on Saturdays he played softball with a team he found through an ad in the LA Weekly. The light blue memo with the telephone number written on it and her name, Lauren, printed across the top stayed on the refrigerator door for three weeks before he called. She sounded pleased to hear his voice, and when he asked to have dinner with him she said she'd love to.

He took her to Musso's. On the way she told him she was divorced from a guy who used to produce a TV show that Bobby had watched once or twice. It was about a couple of surfer buddies who were also cops, a hit for two seasons before it fell apart in the third. Her ex had been generous and the settlement allowed her to pursue her career. She had a commercial running at the moment.

"What's it for?" he asked.

She named a feminine hygiene product.

"I haven't seen it."

"It runs mostly in the daytime during the soaps."

"It figures."

During dinner she told him more about herself. She worked out at the gym five days a week. In addition she took acting classes from a guy Bobby used to know in college. He remembered doing a scene with the actor who sprayed saliva when he talked. Everyone complained about it behind his back.

"He tells me all I have to do is hang in," she

said, "and sooner or later it has to happen."

"That's the beauty part about acting."

"What do you mean?"

"The longer you hang in, the less the competition. Pretty soon you're going up for wheelchair parts, and there're only three of you left to compete."

She reached for her wineglass. "That's grim."

"That's life."

"What about you?"

"What about me?"

"You don't come across like a cab driver."

"How does a cab driver come across?"

"Stop being coy. Were you ever in show business? I'll bet you were."

"I fooled around for a while."

"And?"

"It wasn't in the cards."

"And you don't like to talk about it."

"What's to talk about? It's something that I used to do that I don't do anymore. Like those expensive bad habits."

He managed to keep the conversation on her for the rest of the meal. It wasn't difficult. Actors. They were so easy to figure out. While he ate she talked. He enjoyed listening to her, and she wasn't shy about letting him know she found him attractive. Bobby liked to be stalked. He thought about going to bed with her, and he felt a shift in his shorts. Later, when he pulled up in front of her building she asked him up for a nightcap.

"You can park next to my car, number four. I'll have the doorman open the garage door."

Her apartment was on the tenth floor facing north with a balcony and a view of the hills. The TV producer had indeed been generous. She handed him a beer and excused herself, closing the bedroom door behind her. Bobby sat on the white corduroy sofa and switched on the news. As soon as the picture appeared it was apparent that something big was happening. The screen filled with images of police cars and fire trucks. An on-the-scene reporter, standing in front of the Nine Thousand Building, was informing the TV audience that the SWAT team was now in place. For those who had just tuned in he reported that the police were surrounding a house in the hills above Sunset. Nothing else was known. Viewers were advised to stay tuned.

"Oh, swell," she said from the bedroom door. "I've got an audition first thing tomorrow morning in the Nine Thousand Building. I don't believe this town." They watched for a while until it became apparent that the situation was stalemated. "Would you like to see my commercial?" she asked.

"As a matter of fact, I would."

In the commercial the camera comes up on Lauren and a younger woman riding an escalator while the younger woman confides that she has actually reached a point in her life where she feels confident all the time. When Lauren's character asks her how she did it the younger woman tells her coyly about the product she's been using. Lauren's character just nods and smiles.

"What can I say?" said Bobby. "You look great."

He woke up before sunrise the next morning. She lay curled up in ball on the far side of her king size mattress. He slipped out of the bed and padded across the white carpet to the adjoining bathroom. Returning to the bed he lay on his back and wondered if they would see each other again. The sex had been nice, the way it is when both people expect it to be. The earth hadn't moved, but there was something there, an odds-on chance maybe, that it might move the next time around. It happened without a lot of words. She put on Boz Skaggs and they danced. When he kissed her she took him by the hand and led him to her bed. While he was taking off his shoes she lit a couple of candles on the dresser and turned off the bedside lamps. "I want to undress you," she said.

"I'd like that."

Afterwards, she kissed him and whispered, "You're nice." Then she rolled over away from him. She was asleep in minutes. Now, bladder relieved, he drifted off to sleep again. He dreamed he was at Disneyland with Adam who was acting sullen and uncooperative. Waiting in line at the Pirates Cave Adam bolts off into the crowd. Bobby runs after him frantically calling his name and wondering what he's going to tell Adam's mother. Then Bobby's arms and legs are moving like he's in slow motion, and when he calls out Adam's name no sound comes out. Over the Disneyland loudspeakers they're playing Bobby's recording of L.A. Angel.

He awoke with a start. He was alone in the huge bed. The sliding door to the balcony was open, and sun splashed on the white shag carpet flooding the room with light. He closed his eyes and pulled the pillow over his head enjoying the relief, bordering on bliss, that came when he realized he'd been dreaming. Then he heard the song. He pulled the pillow off his head and sat up to listen. It was his voice all right, and the song was L.A. Angel. It came through the open balcony door. He got up and went outside. The music was originating from the hills up above the Nine Thousand Building, which was visible from the balcony. Suddenly the sliding door from the living room opened, and a heavy set woman carrying a small rug came out. Her eyes met Bobby's and dropped to his cock. He jumped back into the bedroom and pulled on his clothes. She was behind the counter that separated the kitchen from the dining area when he came into the living room. "Would you like a cup of coffee?" she asked.

"Yes, please. What's going on?"

"Up in the hills you mean?"

"Yeah, the music."

"It's all over the TV. Can't get nothin' else. I hope it's over before my programs come on that's all I hope."

He switched on the TV. The FBI, tipped off by an informant, had decided to move in on the members of a para-military cult who were living and stockpiling arms in a Hollywood Hills house. The group got wind of the proposed FBI raid and barricaded themselves. Now they were engaged in a stand-off with the authorities. Part of their defiant stance was to set up stadium size speakers on the roof of the house and to play Bobby's recording over and over at maximum volume. It had been going on since sunrise.

He worked the noon to ten shift that day. His first fare took him far into the Valley to San Fernando. From there he had a radio order to Northridge, and after that he worked Ventura Boulevard until it got dark. He was happy to stay on the Valley side of the hills. According to dispatch the traffic in the city was hopelessly snarled by the closing off of Sunset from West Hollywood to Brentwood. He left the radio off. All the live on-the-scene reports were punctuated by the blaring sound of L.A. Angel in the background, and he couldn't deal with it. Only one fare, his last, a kid headed for the Volvo dealership in Encino, commented on the fracas, not to Bobby but to someone on the other end of a cell phone.

"They sent my mom home from work," said the kid. "She told me Century City looked like a ghost town." The kid listened for a while, and then he asked, "Who the hell is Bobby Spinelli? Bobby tightened his grip on the wheel. The kid let out a hoot. "You're kidding. Stop it, you're pulling my leg." There was another silence followed by a loud laugh. "That is so goddamn funny."

No it's not, thought Bobby, you spoiled little prick.

"OK, dude," said the kid. "Talk to you later." He laughed again.

Bobby pulled to a stop in front of the dealership. "You want me to wait?"

"No. I'm picking up my car."

He decided to call it a day. He called in and told the dispatcher he was coming down with something. At the garage the dispatcher didn't even look when he turned in his medallion. In the office the cashier checked him out without comment. Arriving home, he opened his car door to hear the strains of L.A. Angel coming down from the hills to the north. The Times lay in front of the door to the apartment across the hall. He unlocked his door, looked around to make sure he was alone, and snatched the paper off the welcome mat. Inside his apartment, he leaned against the closed door to look down at the front page. They used an old head shot done when Bobby was twenty. He always hated the picture. Taken too soon after a haircut, it made his ears look large and exposed. For some reason the newspaper had colored the original black and white photo, and Bobby's dark brown hair was given a henna cast making it look like a toupee. The caption read, "Singer of cult anthem never had another hit record." Bobby took a bottle of tequila from the cabinet underneath the kitchen sink and had a long slow pull. Putting the bottle on the coffee table he flopped on the sofa, kicked off his shoes, and read an account of his career, written for laughs by a reporter who was too young to remember Bobby or his era. I don't deserve this, he thought. I never hurt anyone in my whole fucking life, and this isn't fair.

After he put a couple of frozen burritos in the microwave he had another hit of tequila. He checked his voice mail and was relieved to see that he'd forgotten to turn it on. The phone rang a couple of times, but he ignored it. Occasionally he would go to the window, open it, and listen. The music continued to pour down from the hills, unabated. He fell asleep on the sofa before the eleven o'clock news came on waking up in time to see Letterman making his noisy entrance. When the applause died down Letterman showed a clip of the surrounded house in the hills, complete with sound effects. After he cautioned his audience that things could turn ugly out there in LaLa Land, he launched into five minutes of Bobby Spinelli jokes. Bobby felt a wave of nausea roll over him. He checked the medicine cabinet where he found some sleeping pills left behind by a meter maid he used to see. He washed one down with the last of the tequila ignoring the warning on the label. With any luck, he thought as he fell into bed, I'll die in my sleep. He awoke the next morning with a dry mouth and a thundering headache. The telephone was ringing. He pulled the pillow over his head, and let it ring. When it stopped he got out of bed while the events of the previous day flooded back into his consciousness. In the kitchen he stood in front of the open refrigerator door drinking orange juice from the carton when he spied the empty tequila bottle, and a new stab of pain hit his right temple. He turned on the TV. A cartoon came up on the screen, and for a moment his spirit lifted with the possibility that the nightmare was over. But it wasn't over. A channel switch brought back the familiar scene, flashing lights from police cars, the reporter speaking earnestly into the camera, the words Live Action superimposed across the bottom of the screen, and of course the song in the background. There had been a smattering of gun fire during the night. At that point, said the reporter, the cultists turned off the sound barrage to demand safe passage to Chichicastenango.

Oh shit, thought Bobby, now they're calling it a sound barrage. While he was in the shower he decided to get out of town. When he called in to say he'd be out for a day or two he waited for the dispatcher to ask what was wrong. Instead the guy went into a long bitch about having to work a double shift for two days in a row. Bobby hung up the phone. You just think you have problems, buddy boy. He packed a bag with enough clothes for a couple of days, filled a thermos with ice water, and turned on his voice mail. He would have liked to leave it off, but he knew his old man would be calling. A half hour later he was headed north on the Pacific Coast Highway, out of the chaos. He felt better right away.

Grateful for the scenery and for the challenge of the winding road he drove all day stopping only once for fuel and an orange juice. There was very little traffic, and by late afternoon he was in Big Sur. He pulled into a scenic overlook and got out to stretch his legs. As it had often done in the past the ocean pulled him. He locked the car and hopped over the low fence. He crossed a wide meadow and came to a cliff that dropped off to the beach below. The descent was more than he bargained for, and it took him almost a half hour to reach the sand. Sitting on a rock to take off his shoes and socks he saw that he was too far below the cliff to be seen from the road, and he stripped down to his shorts.

He started walking, enjoying the feel of the air on his body. He felt like an alien on an undiscovered planet, a compatible one, but devoid of human life. It felt fine. The only sounds came from the crashing surf and the cries of the birds circling overhead. He wondered again as he had many times what would have happened to him if that goddamn song had never been written. He tried to remember why, when that crazy first year was over, he didn't just pack up and move to New York as he had planned, but it was no use. It was like trying to remember a dream recalled too long after you got out of bed. Dreams weren't his problem now, reality was, the reality of being an object of ridicule, a joke, in a town where only comedians could risk being laughed at. If anyone had asked him what he thought would happen next, or better, why he even cared, he would have been lost for words let alone for ideas. A breaker crashed nearby spraying him with a cold mist that made him shiver. The warmth had gone out of the late afternoon sun. He turned back toward the rock where he had left his clothes.

Later, getting out of the car and walking to the office of a little motel about a mile up the highway he looked at the little cabins and remembered having been there before. It was at least ten years ago, on the way to San Francisco with a lady marine he'd met on a blind date. She was bigger than he was physically, and he had been pleasantly surprised, and more than a bit intrigued, when he realized that the difference didn't faze her. Indeed, it turned her on, and he liked her all the more for that. Driving along with the windows open, the warm breeze blowing her short-cropped red hair, she would reach over occasionally and fondle his cock. By the time they pulled into the motel with its old fashion cabins out back Bobby was ready to explode. In the room the springs on the ancient bed squeaked so loudly that they had to move the mattress to the floor.

"How many nights?" asked the old man behind the desk.

"Just one."

He ate dinner in the coffee shop next to the motel and was in bed asleep by dark. The next morning he stepped out of the cabin and into a cold wet fog. After putting his bag into the trunk of the car he went into the warm coffee shop. It was empty except for two men in plaid shirts seated at one of the small tables and a ranger at the cash register paying for a coffee to go. Bobby sat at the counter and ordered bacon and eggs from a woman whom he guessed was the proprietor's wife. While she prepared his breakfast he listened to the music from a small radio on the shelf between the kitchen and the dining room. "Did you say over on these eggs?" she asked.

"No, up." Just then the music stopped and the news came on. Bobby tensed and stayed like that, almost coiled, while he listened to the announcer read what was happening on the world scene. Then it came.

"In Los Angeles, the two day confrontation between police and a self-proclaimed freedom fighter group came to an end just before midnight last night when the insurgents surrendered to the police without a battle to the death as they had threatened. There were no fatalities in the stand-off which played havoc with traffic in the Southern California metropolis."

The woman served the bacon and eggs. "You want more coffee?"

"Please."

"Now for a report on highway conditions," said the announcer, "we go to Joe O'Donnell."

After breakfast he got into his car and headed south. He crossed the county line in mid-afternoon. The broad beaches north of the city were mostly deserted except for the weekday die-hards. There was no wind and hardly any surf. The pale sand rested flat and still as it waited in the hot sun. Off shore the surfers, floating on their boards like flotsam, waited too. He stopped in a super market in Malibu to buy a six pack and some frozen lasagna. Once he'd seen Sting in that market. Bobby had turned into one of the aisles, and there he was standing next to a crammed shopping cart reading the label on a jar of nuts. Bobby avoided looking at him. He remembered how flattering it was at first to be recognized and stared at and how quickly it became a meaningless annoyance.

Outside the store he looked at his watch. He had made good time. He turned off the Coast Highway at the Sunset Boulevard intersection and followed the long meandering road through the Brentwood hills into West Hollywood. He drove by the Nine Thousand Building. There was no evidence of the recent high drama that had surrounded it. People were coming and going through the glass doors, and traffic flowed by it as if the building weren't there. He thought about

Lauren and wondered how her audition had gone. There was a parking place right in front of his building. Maybe my luck is changing he thought. The kid next door, wearing a neck brace, watched while Bobby opened the trunk and removed his bag.

"You been away?" asked the kid.

"Yeah."

"Where'd you go?"

"Minneapolis."

"What for?"

"Visiting friends. What happened to your neck?"

"Me and my mom got rear ended in the Beverly Center Garage. We're suing."

"Good luck."

"Thanks."

The stuffy air in the apartment smelled like tequila and he hurriedly threw open the windows. He put the beer and the lasagna in the refrigerator and went into the bedroom to unpack his bag. After he took a shower and put on a pair of jeans and a tee shirt he watered the plants. He opened a can of beer and put the lasagna in the oven. The sound of someone practicing scales on a piano came through the window from the house next door. When he finished eating he sat back and stared at the blinking light on his telephone. It was time to pick up his voice mail. The first two messages were hang ups. Then a voice identified herself as a reporter for Eye Witness News. She left a number for him to call no matter what time he got in. Next there was another reporter, this one from National Public Radio asking for a telephone interview and promising it would take no more than ten minutes. Someone from the office of Joel Nachman at the William Morris Agency left a callback number. Next he heard his old man's voice, shaky with age and nervous talking to a machine, asking Bobby to call him in Hemet, where he lived alone, retired. Then the voice of Joel Nachman himself saying it was important. Then Lauren's throaty tones, "You really are a mystery man. I remember your record. I saw you sing it on the Bob Hope Show when I was in high school. Nachman's voice came on again, this time slightly agitated. He could get Bobby two weeks at the Villa Capri in Oxnard at fifteen hundred a week, but they had to act fast. After Nachman there was another hang up and then three reporters in a row from local TV stations. Finally Nachman again, frantic now, saying that unless he heard from Bobby within the hour the deal was blown.

Bobby dialed his father.

"Where were you?" asked the old man. "I called you yesterday morning. They were talking about you on Good Morning America."

"I've been away. Is everything all right?"

"Never mind me. What is all this about? Your picture was in the paper."

"You know as much as I do. They played the song to annoy the cops, I guess."

"People out here were asking me. I didn't know what to say. I felt like a goddamn horse's ass."

"Dad, I'm sorry. I didn't have anything to do with it."

"Are they allowed to do that? Just play your record over and over?"

"I don't think they asked anyone."

"I'm glad your mother wasn't around to see this, may she rest in peace, it would kill her."

"Dad, it's over."

"When am I going to see you? You'd think Hemet was on the East Coast."

"I'll be out one of these weekends."

"Are you still driving a cab?"

"You know I am."

"You had talent, Bobby. You were as good as Vic Damone."

"I have to go. Take care of yourself, OK?

"Don't be a stranger."

"Goodnight, Dad."

"Goodnight."

Bobby hung up the phone. Then he went to the refrigerator for another beer and turned out the lights. Sitting in the darkness he listened to the wind rustling the leaves of the tree outside his window while the shadows of its leaves, cast there by the streetlight, danced on the living room wall.

OSCAR

N o diet soda," said my brother. "I don't know why I bother to look."

He slammed the refrigerator door shaking loose a snapshot of Al Pacino held there by a soft plastic magnet made to look like a slice of pepperoni. I took the picture myself years ago in New York when Al and I were in the same acting class. My brother gave me the magnet. The store he works at near the Santa Monica pier sells them.

"There's orange juice," I said.

"You know orange juice gives me hives. Jesus."

"Drink water, then."

"Fuck you."

He had a major burn going. He must have seen the morning paper. Squeezing past me in the narrow kitchen, his huge stomach forcing me against the sink, he limped into the living room where he dropped heavily into the sturdy leather chair I maintain for his use. "Are you still planning to have an Oscar party?" he asked.

"I haven't decided yet. I thought I'd wait until the nominations are in before I go ahead."

"When is that supposed to happen?" I was sure

he knew. He reads Variety.

"At the end of the week," I said. We're identical twins, and we have our own way of communicating. "What's happening with you?"

"My landlord wants to paint."

"So?"

"It will mean a rent raise."

"It usually does."

"Just so you know."

I had been surprised to see him waiting for me when I came home that evening. He usually stays away when I'm working. I had been looking forward to an uneventful evening, alone.

"You sound like you have a cold," he said while we were eating dinner.

"No. It's my sinuses. My scenes are outdoors in the hills and the pollen count is way up."

"Is it a western?

"God no. What would I do in a western?"

"How would I know?' He helped himself to the last of the chili. "You and those sinuses. Why don't I have sinus trouble? You'd think on top of everything else I would have gotten sinus trouble, too." I didn' t answer him. We continued to eat in silence, our gaze drifting back and forth between our food and CNN on the TV screen. The sound was muted, a preference I acquired during the Vietnam War when the noise of battle tended to make my stomach tense. Nowadays with battles raging on every street corner all over the world I continue to handle stress with the mute key.

"Why don't you just switch it off altogether and listen to music?" he asked. "That's what I do. I listen to Broadway show tunes."

"I don't like to listen to Broadway show tunes."

"There are other kinds of music, you know."

"I'd rather watch the news with the sound turned off."

"You're weird."

Look whose talking. For dessert I offered him the apple turnover I'd bought on the way home from the studio.

He started eating as soon as I put it in front of him. "Aren't you having one?"

"No. I ate a candy bar today. That's enough sugar."

He put down the fork and pushed away the turnover without comment.

"I hate to kick you out," I said, but I've got some lines to learn."

"I wasn't planning on staying. I have to go in early. We're taking inventory. I not only have to sell that shit, I have to count it too."

I used to tell him to look for another job when he talked like that, but I don't anymore. After he left I put the dishes in the dishwasher and studied my lines. Most of the stuff for the next day was action, so it didn't take long. I make a nice living playing characters that support the leads without shifting the focus away from them. The trick is to be innocuous and integral at the same time. Occasionally, if you're lucky, you can make a part like that memorable. That happened to me last year when I was cast in an action picture as a hotel clerk who witnesses a murder. There's a scene where my character gets grilled by a detective who's sure he did it. The detective had the star part, so I figured that the nearest I'd get to a close up would be a tight two shot. Well go figure. They shot the scene with my face filling the screen for a two-minute monolog that every critic mentioned with a rave. It was enough to get me my next job without an audition. I thought I'd seen the end of it until Variety ran a front page article, the one I was sure my brother saw but wasn't mentioning, citing me as a contender for an Oscar nomination.

Any actor who tells you that he or she never thinks about winning an Oscar is lying. I know I've had a fantasy or two about running down that aisle and up onto that stage into the open arms of last year's winner. I even have an acceptance speech that I put together mentally one night thirty-five years ago on the E train stalled in the tunnel under the East River during a power failure. Given the type of career I have, though, I spend most of the time thinking about what, if anything, I'm going to be doing when I finish the job I'm on. I once went two years without working, and to this day I don't know why. I just couldn't seem to go up for anything with my name on it. It was the worst period of my life, and I thought it would never end. It did end of course, it always does, and now here I was a contender for an Oscar nomination. I love show business.

The next day, when I came home from work there was a voice mail from my brother asking me to call him at work.

"What's up?"

"I need you to go over to my place and give Eydie her insulin shot."

Eydie is one of his cats. She has diabetes. I told him I would.

"I have to be here until at least midnight," he said. "Maybe later the way things are going."

"Why?"

"Because a fucking pipe burst in the stockroom, that's why, and the dragon lady has got us wading around in a foot of water trying to save the worthless crap she unloads on the turistas."

"Hasn't she got insurance?"

"What do I know? I'm just a clerk. I do what I'm told. Look, I know you hate doing this, but she'll go into shock if she has to wait until I get home."

"It's nobody's fault."

"Feed them too. All the stuff is in the kitchen cabinet under the sink."

"I know. Try not to get too damp."

"Have a good laugh." He hung up without saying goodbye. He's the only person I know with absolutely no sense of humor.

I drove to his apartment and let myself in. Steve, the other cat, choosing not to acknowledge my presence, sat like a black Buddha under the coffee table. He's the biggest cat I've ever seen. In addition to having an abnormally large frame he's a good ten pounds overweight. I once suggested to my brother that he submit Steve's statistics to the Guinness Book of World Records.

"He's got an overactive thyroid, for chrissake. Just because you can eat anything you want without gaining an ounce you think obesity is a joke."

"I wasn't suggesting you put him on a diet."

"I can't put him on a diet."

"Why?"

"Think about it. He doesn't know what a goddamn diet is. He'd only know that I was starving him. It would be cruel."

While Steve was eating I filled a syringe and went looking for Eydie. As small and dainty as Steve is large and clumsy, she was hiding under my brother's huge bed among the bundles of Playbills he stores there. Long resigned to the daily insulin shot she submitted to the needle, but grudgingly. Neither of the cats is overly fond of me. As soon as I released her she went back to her place among the Playbills. When we lived in New York, before I got into the movies, my brother used to go to the theater a lot, and he always saved the Playbill. He planned to have the covers framed someday.

"Why?" I asked.

"So I can hang them on a wall of course."

"All of them?"

"Why not?"

"I think it's a bit much."

"I think you're a bit much."

Before I left the bedroom I looked in his closet. His jackets, pants, and shirts were arranged by color. His shoes were in neat rows on the floor, the left regular the right ones prosthetic. My closet is identical, except I'm four sizes smaller, and I don't have any prosthetic shoes. He was the second born and a breech birth. They had to use forceps and in the process his left foot was crushed. In the bathroom I checked out the medicine cabinet, reading the labels on all the prescriptions. He takes a lot of meds. In the living room I went through his CDs to see if he had anything new. He collects original cast recordings. On the way out I noticed that I'd left the front door open. It's not the kind of thing I normally do, but I'd been day dreaming a lot lately since the article about the contenders came out.

I tried not to dwell on it, but it was hard not to. Everyone on the set made a big deal of it, and even my agent called to wish me luck. The local media were starting to come down with Oscar fever. Driving home on the freeway I listened to a talk show whose guest was an actor I know. The host asked him what a nomination would mean to him, personally. He said all the usual things about how it would be very encouraging and how it would boost his price a notch or two. That's about what I would have said. The big difference between him and me, however, was that he could experience it singly. His joy would be shaped only by his own sensibility, unlike mine would be. I tried to imagine what it would be like to live without a congenital compulsion to share, to compete without the inhibiting requirement to keep things even, to advance oneself without causing pain to another, to feel whole instead of half. It was useless. It was like trying to imagine having wings and flying. could picture it of course, but by virtue of my fate I couldn't feel it. When I got home I found a message from the studio telling me the shooting schedule had been altered and I had the next day off. I turned in early anyway. I was asleep for a couple of hours when I was awakened by the phone. It was my brother. He was beside himself.

"Steve is gone," he said.

"What do you mean?"

"Jesus Christ, shall I try it in French? He's gone. He's nowhere in the apartment. I've looked everywhere."

"What time is it?"

"Don't you have a fucking clock? It's quarter to one."

"You're sure he's gone?"

"Give me a little credit, would you? Do you really think I'd be calling you like this if I weren't sure?"

"I was thinking he might be hiding someplace."

"Eydie hides. Steve doesn't hide. You know that. Jesus."

"What are you going to do?"

"I don't know what to do. I can't think."

"Calm down. We'll think of something."

"How did he act when you were here?"

"The way he always acts."

"What do you mean?"

"Like he hadn't had anything to eat for a week."

"That's it. Start making cracks about his goddamn appetite. That's just what I need to hear."

"Where could he be?"

"You saw him last. You tell me."

All of a sudden I remembered the front door. He must have run out while I was snooping around. My stomach sank. "Do you want me to come over?"

"Would you?"

"I'll be there as soon as I can."

He was standing in front of his building smoking a cigarette when I got there. He stepped on it hastily when he saw me.

"I think we should drive around the neighborhood," he said.

"OK. Get in."

He has to do a bit of maneuvering to get in and

out of my car, tuning sideways, lowering himself into the seat, then turning towards the front while he pulls his legs in, one at a time. "These goddamn bucket seats," he said.

"When did you start smoking again?"

"Could we talk about it some other time? All I can think about now is that cat alone out there in the dark."

"I left the door ajar when I was here. He must have gotten out then."

"I figured that."

"I've had a lot on my mind."

"Stop down at the end of the street. We can start there." He still hadn't mentioned anything about the Oscars.

We drove around for an hour, stopping periodically to call Steve's name through the rolled down windows. I couldn't help it, every time I peered off into the darkness I'd picture him out there in all his big black bulk hearing us calling and waiting obstinately, eyes narrowing the way cat's eyes do. He barely tolerated me, so it was easy to imagine him hearing my voice, perversely pleased with the disruption he was causing. "I think we should call it a day," I said.

"And do what?"

"Tomorrow we can get in touch with those people who find lost pets. I forget what they call themselves. You pay a fee and they put up posters with the cat's picture on them. They advertise, too, I think, in the local papers."

"I'm not sure I've got a decent picture of him by himself. I always seem to take him and Eydie together."

"You probably don't even need a picture, you can get away with just describing him."

"What do you mean?"

"Face it. He's not your average looking cat."

"You can't let that go, can you?"

"It's been a long day."

I slept in the following morning and went to the gym in the afternoon. The guy at the desk wished me good luck. The nominations were due in two days. I tried to keep it in perspective, but when I allowed myself to think about it I wanted it so badly it hurt. When I left the gym I drove to my brother's place to give Eydie her insulin. He was working late again that night. He'd engaged the pet finding people and already the telephone poles in his neighborhood were displaying yellow notices. There was no picture, only the words, extra large black cat answers to the name of Steve, in bold letters along with my brother's telephone number. By the next day, the day before the announcements, there was still no sign of Steve. I had a night scene on location at the County Museum of Art, so I didn't get home until late. My brother was out when I called. I left him a voice mail saying that I had an early call. I asked him not to wake me up unless it was necessary.

I didn't get a nomination. The big news for those who did was on the front page of the Times and, in case anyone might have missed it, repeated every half hour on the TV news shows. Before I left for the studio my agent called to tell me I was up for a nice part in a mini-series about a serial killer, You win a few, you lose a few. It's no more complicated than that.

Three weeks to the day after Steve disappeared my brother was watering the shrubberies around his steps when he saw what he thought was a huge black rat staggering up the front walk.

"I'll never forget that sight as long as I live," he said. "He was nothing but bones. His coat hung on him a blanket thrown over a stack of kindling wood."

"A big stack of kindling wood."

"I cannot fucking believe you said that."

"Where do you think he was?"

"The vet thinks he was probably trapped in an abandoned building, maybe a garage that someone closed the door of after he got inside. He's suffering from severe dehydration. They said he had to stay in the hospital for at least a week. I don't even want to think what it's going to cost."

"What's the alternative?"

"I'm just letting you know."

"I've decided to have a few people over for dinner and to watch the Oscar ceremony. You're invited too, of course."

"God, I can't believe it's Oscar time again." He

sounded uncharacteristically happy.

As always when I invited him to one of my parties I hoped he would have something else to do, but he never did. It isn't easy being at a party with him, something I learned a long time ago. When we were kids our parents used to like to show us off, dressing us alike and urging us to perform whenever they had company. We were both natural hams, so it didn't take a lot of urging on their part. We used to sing Every Street's A Boulevard In Old New York, and I worked out a little two step that I did moving in a circle around him. One time when I was really getting into the dance part he just stopped singing and clumped out of the room leaving me there alone, surrounded by relatives, to continue solo. I did of course, but I stopped dancing, and while I was finishing the song I gave way to the feelings of resentment that were to grow like a tumor in the fiber of my being. We were both injured. My brother's injury, as tragic and immutable as it is, is on the surface to be seen and commiserated with. Mine is deeper than that, and I have to bear it alone.

AMOR FATI

The aerator in the aquarium was off. Brian knew something was wrong in the living room as soon as he let himself in the front door. It was only when he was putting the mail on the table where the tank sat that he missed the bubbling sound. He flipped on the light switch to see if there was any power. The lamp on the table next to the sofa came on. Then he saw what the trouble was. The aerator plug had come out of the wall socket. He reinserted it, and the fluorescent light that ran along the top rim of the tank flickered on. If the fish noticed the light or the sudden influx of oxygen from the windows of the small castle on the floor of their home they showed no sign of it, much less of any gratitude toward their benefactor. That was the problem with fish as far as Brian was concerned. They never gave anything in return. Julie, his wife, didn't seem to mind that, and when she fed them daily and cleaned their tank every Saturday she always looked as if she was on the brink of a smile. Brian called it her look of quiet pleasure, and he found it very engaging, even if he could take or leave the fish.

Julie's look of quiet pleasure was much in evidence lately now that their lives had changed so drastically. For the first time in the seven years they'd been married he had a regular job, and they were trying to get pregnant. That was the way Julie put it when she mentioned it to friends. It had been a long day, and he was glad the weekend was here. He worked as a trainee in a large insurance company in the Mid-Wilshire district, and a lot of his energy went into looking busy. Today there had been a long trainee meeting with a vice-president from the New York office. The meeting ran into the lunch hour, and the vice-president, flattered by the barrage of questions thrown at him, suggested that they send out for sandwiches and make it a working lunch. Brian invented a dentist appointment and hurried away to his tap dancing lesson at the Mario del Farco School of the Dance on Third near Western.

Leaving his jacket and tie in the car he took his tap shoes out of the trunk and hurried in past Mr. del Farco's office on the first floor up the stairs to the mirror-lined studio on the second. The class fluctuated between ten and fifteen students, most of them actors. Brian was a musician, keyboard, before his job change.

The tap dancing class was originally a form of physiotherapy suggested by his doctor to help rehabilitate his right leg broken in an automobile accident. He and the other five members of the band he used to play in were returning from a gig in San Luis Obispo when Joey Garagliano the drummer fell asleep at the wheel. The van rolled over in a ditch. Everyone except Brian got away with minor injuries.

He spent two months in traction, most of it in a rented hospital bed in the spare room of the bungalow he and Julie rented in Santa Monica, two blocks from the beach. Except for a dull ache on damp days, the leg was mended. He continued with the tap lessons, because he enjoyed the challenge.

In the studio, Mr. del Farco was demonstrating an arm movement to Nola Weisbart, a plump large breasted woman in a black leotard. He stood behind her manipulating her arms, his small supple body spooned against her broad back. Nola looked uncomfortable. Brian changed into his tap shoes while he mentally reviewed the dance steps he had been practicing. The class was working on a military-style close order routine, and as usual he hadn't practiced enough. There was no place at home to do it except the narrow sidewalk in their tiny front yard, and no matter what time of the day or night he went out there to go over the increasingly intricate stuff del Farco was laying on them the little girl next door would appear in the window of her house, rest her arms on the sill, put her thumb in her mouth, and stare at him.

"I would think you'd like an audience," said Julie.

"She doesn't look like she approves."

The meeting was still going on when he got back to the office, and it lasted until four fifteen. The training director told them all to go home early. Brian called Julie at work to tell her he'd do the grocery shopping. He went to Gelson's in Century City. Julie liked their potato salad. At home, he put away the groceries and changed into jeans. Barefoot and shirtless he wheeled the grill out from under the back porch and filled it with charcoal. Then he sat down on the back porch step and lit up a joint. He could hear Tessa, their neighbor from the house next door, singing along with James Taylor. She was a legal secretary who had just been fired after a tumultuous affair with her married boss. Now she was trying to establish her own business as a numerologist.

"It's weird," she told Julie and Brian one night when they sat in the darkness of the back yard drinking wine and talking about themselves, "I've lost two other jobs in the past three years for the same reason, and I'm not that wild about sex."

"Why do you do it?" asked Julie.

"I don't know," said Tessa.

Julie, who worked as a researcher for a psychology journal, thought Tessa was a flake whose behavior was typical of what Julie called, the beach syndrome. "Instant gratification is a large part of it," she told Brian, "and a tendency to see life solely as something to be enjoyed."

Tessa called through her kitchen window screen. "Is that you, Brian?"

"Yes."

"Is that weed I smell?"

"Yes again. You want some?"

"No, but I could do a glass of wine."

"Come on over."

He went up the back stairs to the kitchen and opened one of the two bottles he'd brought home. When he returned to the back yard she was sitting in one of the lawn chairs. He handed her the glass. "I hope you like cabernet."

"What's not to like? Cheers."

"What did I do with that joint?"

"It's probably in the house."

He took the steps two at a time. The joint was on the kitchen windowsill. It had gone out. He dropped it into a small dish on the counter and rejoined Tessa. "So how's business?"

"I did two charts last week. Not enough to pay the rent, but I took an ad in the numerology newsletter, so we'll see. I'm almost finished with yours."

"And?"

"You have a tendency to be easily led."

"That's a good quality in a musician."

"It's like everything else. It's neither good nor bad. It's what you do with it."

"Is that heavy, or is it just because I'm a little stoned?"

"Some of both, probably."

A telephone rang.

"That's ours," said Brian. It was Julie to tell him she had to work late and to remind him that today was a fertile day.

"Oh shit, I just masturbated."

"You've got to be kidding."

"I'm kidding." After he hung up he returned to the backyard where Tessa was pulling weeds from the small flower garden outside her door. "I'm going for a walk on the beach," he called.

"Enjoy," she said.

In the house he put on a sweatshirt and looked for his sneakers under the bed. Then he remembered they were in the living room on the floor at the end of the sofa where he'd kicked them off last night when he lay down to watch L.A Law. He'd fallen asleep before it was over. He couldn't stay awake past ten these days. When he was playing with the band he rarely got to bed before dawn.

At the beach the ocean sky was gray and the sun artificially pink through the fog that was blowing in off the water. His walks on the beach like his bed time had changed when he left the band. He used to walk north and gaze out toward Malibu fantasizing about the life they'd have there when the band hit it big. The house with a studio attached would be right on the beach. He'd compose all day, and then they'd go for a run before dinner, barefoot, zigzagging at the edge of the changing water line. Nowadays he tended to walk south, away from Malibu, toward the breakwater that separated Santa Monica from Venice. Today the beach was deserted for the most part, settled into its chilly winter mode. Halfway to the breakwater he sat down to watch the sun disappear. As the pink sliver dropped out of sight he thought about where it would be now in the Hawaiian sky.

He loved the scenery in the Islands. Julie's parents had given them a trip there last year for an anniversary present. It was on the balcony of their hotel room in Maui that she told him she couldn't live any more the way they had been living. She said she loved him, but she needed a husband who ate and slept at the same times she did. She was tired of weekends alone, playing volleyball on the beach and coming home to dinner for one while he was off on a gig. Furthermore, she said, it was time to start making some specific plans about a baby, before it was too late. That meant giving up her job for a couple of years. Music had never paid him enough to support them both, and it was anyone's guess when and if it ever would. Listening to her that day on the balcony, the Trade Winds blowing the curtains of the room behind them, he realized that while he wasn't looking their dreams had gone off in different directions, and holding on to his would cost him a marriage. He wasn't sure he was willing to give up his dreams, but he didn't want to lose her. He was sure of that. Until he met her his life had lacked meaning. She had given it that. She calmed his fears. She represented sanity in an insane world. He told her he'd get a straight job.

It was dark by the time he got back from the

beach. He decided to finish the joint before Julie got home. She didn't approve of it ever since the counselor in the fertility clinic told them it lowered the sperm count. Brian's sperm count, monitored several times in the past months, remained high, so he tended to discount Julie's concern. She had gone off the pill as soon as he got the job with the insurance company. When she failed to conceive after a couple of months she insisted that they enroll in the fertility clinic. Their love making which had always been spontaneous and, because of their disparate schedules, not subject to any time frame, became something else. Brian began to think of it as making a deposit, an expression used by the receptionist in a Greenpeace tee shirt when she handed him a sterile jar and pointed to a small room down the hall. It was there in that chilly cubicle that he first experienced performance anxiety, an idea the counselor identified and planted in Brian's mind on their first visit. Until then the idea of such a thing had never crossed his mind, but then, as he sat back in the paper covered armchair, his trousers and under shorts down around his ankles, he stared at the empty receptacle resting on a nearby table and watched it lose its identity as a jar and take on all the aspects of a challenge. When he finished he left the jar on the table as he had been instructed to do, and departed, avoiding the receptionist's eyes.

He was folding the laundry when he heard Julie open the front door.

"Hi," she called.

He joined her in the living room. "Hi."

She came into his arms and kissed him, holding her lips on his and caressing the back of his neck the way he liked. "You've been smoking," she said into his mouth.

He released her. "Give me a break. I've got so many sperm they're running down my leg, and besides, it's Friday."

"The aerator's working?"

"It was unplugged."

"I know. I unplugged it this morning. It was making a funny noise."

"It must have been a short-term virus."

She sat down and kicked off her shoes. "Shall we go out to eat?"

The telephone rang before he could answer. It was his best friend Chickie, the lead singer in the band. Chickie and his wife Bonnie were in the neighborhood and wanted to stop by. Brian told them to come ahead.

"I can't believe you did that," said Julie.

"I'm sorry. I haven't seen him for over a month. I wasn't thinking. Maybe they won't stay."

"That would be a first." She went into the bedroom carrying her shoes. "And you can bet they'll have Mordecai with them."

"He's still nursing. They have to keep him with them."

"Don't you think it's odd," she called from the bedroom, "nursing a two year old kid?"

"Chickie has a theory that most of his problems stem from being weaned too soon."

She came back into the living room. "That and the two tons of dope he's smoked."

"He doesn't do drugs anymore."

"I guess we'd better wait to see if they've eaten." She opened the refrigerator door. "What did you buy?"

"Everything. We can do hamburgers on the grill."

She closed the refrigerator door. "This is not the evening I had planned."

Another thing Brian found engaging about his wife was her ability to acquiesce gracefully to the inevitable. He remembered an instructor in a philosophy seminar who said that accepting one's fate was the secret of happiness. The instructor, a doctoral candidate later dismissed for sexual harassment, called it amor fati. Brian wondered how you recognized your fate. He discussed it with Julie.

"If you're doing it," she said, "it's your fate."

Their guests arrived while he was in the back yard lighting the coals. Chickie came down the back stairs holding Mordecai whose bottom half was naked. He put his son down on the grass and hugged Brian. "Hey Sport."

"Hey yourself. Where have you been?"

"We went up to visit Bonnie's folks for a week,

and the band had a gig in Bishop during that Mule Days thing they have there."

"How did it go?"

"What, the visit with my in-laws or the Mule Days thing?"

Brian laughed. "Both."

"Put it this way. After a week with my father-inlaw, I was ready for Bishop. I never saw so much mule shit, though. God, I'm glad we live in the age of the automobile."

"You want something to drink?"

"Julie's pouring me a glass of wine. How's the insurance business?"

"Good. Two more months in the training program and I get assigned to a department."

Chickie didn't respond.

Brian nodded towards Mordecai who was exploring under the porch where they kept the beach stuff. "Did you run out of diapers?"

"No, he has a touch of diaper rash, and Bonnie wants to expose his butt to the air for a little while."

"What if he let's go?"

"We duck and hope he's not around food."

Brian laughed again. Chickie had been making him laugh since they were roommates in college whose bond was sealed from the beginning by music. Chickie played the trumpet, but he restricted himself to singing when they formed the band in their junior year.

"You'll stay for dinner, I hope."

"Thanks. Julie asked us, too. We were hoping you would."

There was a crash from under the porch. Mordecai had pulled over a stack of folded metal chairs. Startled but unhurt, he let out a wail. Chickie picked him up. "Jesus, I'll be glad when this kid goes to college."

In the kitchen, Julie was making a salad while Bonnie sculpted hamburgers. Chickie put Mordecai under the table and dumped his blocks. Brian kissed Bonnie on the cheek.

"It's none of my business," said Julie, "but why isn't Mordecai circumcised?"

"No," said Brian, "it isn't."

"Don't be silly," said Bonnie. "It's a perfectly natural question. Mordecai is probably going to be asked it for the rest of his life.   It was Chickie's idea. Ask him."

"If we weren't supposed to have a foreskin," said Chickie, "we wouldn't have been born with one. I've always resented my parents' depriving me of mine."

"Aside from the fact that he's Jewish, they say it's more hygienic," said Julie.

"Who are, they?" asked Chickie

"The medical establishment," said Bonnie.

"Right," said Chickie, "and they're not even thinking about the money they make on it."

"My uncle was the obstetrician, and he didn't

charge us."

"He can always get it done himself later on if it's what he wants."

"When it's major surgery." said Bonnie. "I keep telling you, that's what parenting is, making choices. That implies the possibility of not always making the correct ones."

"That's scary," said Brian.

Julie looked at him over the salad bowl. "No it isn't. It's reality."

"Who wants more wine?" asked Brian.

At dinner Chickie announced that the band had been taken on by a new manager who was famous in the business for having steered a couple of well known groups into the large income bracket. Julie proposed a toast. After he drank Brian tried to ignore the sinking feeling in his chest. He watched Mordecai, in his playpen now and wearing a diaper, point his little finger at the aquarium and babble at the fish.

What do you suppose he's saying?" asked Julie.

"I'd like to think it's something brilliant," said Bonnie, "but Chickie says it's just noise."

"Maybe it's a language you bring into the world with you," said Brian, "one that you forget the longer you're here."

"I like that," said Chickie. "Maybe that's what music is, a language we bring with us. It would help to explain why Mozart was able to compose at such an early age."

"If that were so," said Julie, "wouldn't there be a lot more child prodigies?"

"Not necessarily," said Brian. "Maybe what separates the genius from the rest of us is that the genius remembers."

Chickie sniffed. "I know one thing, Amadeus there has pooped his pants. Where's the diaper bag?"

After dinner they listened to some cuts from the demo the band was working on. After the last one Bonnie said they'd better get going. Julie stood, too quickly Brian thought, and went to get a present for Mordecai that they'd been holding since his birthday last month. Chickie folded the playpen, rounded up the toys, and threw the diaper bag over his shoulder. "We can't just be someplace anymore," he said. "We have to create an environment first."

Bonnie shifted Mordecai to her other hip. "We can't send him back."

"I'm not complaining. I'm explaining," said Chickie.

Brian and Julie walked them to the car and waited for Chickie to put Mordecai's things in the trunk.

"Stay in touch," said Brian as Chickie pulled the door closed.

"Yeah," said Chickie. When he turned the key there was a click. He tried again. Another click.

"Oh, no," said Julie.

"Is it the battery?" asked Brian. "I've got jumper

cables."

"No," said Bonnie, "it's the starter. I've told him fifteen times in the past two weeks. The mechanic said it could go anytime."

"Then he quoted the price of a new one," said Chickie, "plus labor."

"Shit," said Bonnie.

"Shit," said Mordecai.

"Nice talk, mother," said Chickie.

"I'll take you home," said Brian. "Put your stuff in my car." He followed Julie into the house to get the keys. "Come with me."

"I'm really not in the mood for getting back on to the freeway."

He picked up the keys from the dresser and went into the kitchen where she was loading the dishwasher. "I won't be long."

She didn't answer.

"Are you upset?"

"Let's just say I'm confused."

"Why?"

"Go. I can hear Mordecai crying."

"See you later." On the way out he heard a glass shatter on the kitchen floor.

"Shit," she said softly. She rarely said that.

Chickie and Bonnie snapped at each other all the way to West Hollywood, and Brian was happy to leave them after he helped Chickie unload the car.

"I'll call you tomorrow," said Chickie, "after I

talk to the Automobile Club."

The house was dark when Brian got home except for the light on the front porch and the one in the aquarium. He brushed his teeth and undressed in the bathroom. He got into bed without turning on a light. Julie lay with her back to him. He could tell she was awake, and he waited for her to acknowledge him or at least to move. Instead she drifted off, and soon the dark silence became even more silent, broken only by the sound of her slow, even breathing and from the living room, the bubbling of the aerator.

DIAMOND HEAD

He was sitting on the sofa when Serena got home from school. He was like a lot of the other men her mother went on dates with, good looking, shiny shampooed hair, and clean hands with manicured fingernails. For Serena it was mainly the fingernails that set these men apart from her uncles, her mother's brothers, who worked with their hands in the dirt all day pulling vegetables from the ground. This one, whose name was Ron, had been seeing her mother for a couple of months. Tonight he was taking her for dinner on his boat. Serena could hear her in the bedroom hurrying around getting ready. Today was her mother's day off from the shop where she cut and styled men's hair, where she met the men she went out with.

I thought we were supposed to go to a movie and have dinner.

Oh honey, I got my dates mixed up.

She told Serena that Ron had a lot of money, that he had homes in Beverly Hills, Aspen, and Miami. When she got to know Ron better she was going to ask him if they could use his address in Beverly Hills so Serena could to a school there.

Be nice to him Serena.

She waited for Ron to ask her how school was. They always did that, these men of her mother's, even though they weren't really interested.

How's school?

Good.

Junior high next year, huh?

She nodded.

Her mother came in filling the room with the scent of the honey cocomango body lotion she used. She had on white shorts and a pale yellow shirt that showed off her dark beauty. Serena was fair, with light brown hair and blue eyes.

Like your father.

Did my father have clean fingernails?

What are you talking about? Of course he did.

In the kitchen, her mother gave her twenty dollars in case she wanted to have a pizza delivered.

I know you're disappointed, but try to understand. I'm doing this for you.

She always said that. It's for you, Serena. What did she mean? Did she take money from the men, like a *puta*? Once Serena heard her uncle call her mother, his sister, that. Serena's friend Alicia from Confirmation class told her it was a woman who took money from men.

We'll go to a movie over the weekend. We'll have lunch in a restaurant after Mass and go.

After Ron and her mother left she watched TV for a while. It was a movie about a nun who was stranded on a desert island with a soldier. Serena had thought about becoming a nun. When she told Sister

Lucia, her fifth grade teacher last year, Sister's eyes filled up and she hugged Serena. Sister Lucia mentioned it to Sister Josephine who taught music, and Sister Josephine told several of the nuns including Sister Frances who was Serena's teacher now in the sixth grade. The truth was, though, that soon after she told Sister Lucia she changed her mind. She would become a nurse instead. Would the nuns love her less if she became a nurse? She couldn't risk it. She kept her plans to herself. It wasn't a lie, she didn't have to confess, it was the truth when she said it. That's all that counted. Her mother told her that sometimes it was OK to lie, if you had to. Sometimes a lie was the only thing that could help you when you had to have help. That's not what Father Leo said in Catechism class when Serena asked him.

When the movie was over she put the TV on mute and picked up the book that she had taken out of the library for a geography book report on Hawaii. It turned out to be the wrong book for what she needed, being mostly about Honolulu and written for tourists. She had gotten interested in it anyway and had read all but ten pages. She finished them off now and decided to have a bath. While she was filling the tub she heard the couple from the apartment next door opening their front door. They were arguing as usual. She hoped they weren't getting ready for a fight. Twice in the past month the neighbors had called the police. When the tub was filled she got in and lay back in the warm water resting her head on the air-filled neck pillow she'd given her mother for Christmas. She stared at the water stain on the ceiling. The landlord told them the pipes from the upstairs apartment had leaked. He said he'd have the ceiling repainted. That was six months ago.

She hated the apartment. The living room window looked out onto a long balcony that gave access to all the apartments on the second floor. Anyone walking by could look right into the living room. Once while doing her homework she looked up to see a man standing there looking at her. She had never been so frightened. Since then they kept the blinds closed all the time depriving themselves of even the small amount of sunlight that used to come through the window. The apartments in the building surrounded a courtyard with a small swimming pool that didn't look clean. No one ever swam in it. The place seemed nicer three years ago when they moved in, but maybe she only imagined that. Maybe she just didn't notice it, because she was so happy to be with her mother at last. They had never lived together before they moved here. Serena lived up north with her grandparents from the time she was born until her mother finally came to get her.

Why did you leave me?

There was nothing else I could do. I had to get away from there. I was a young girl when you were born. Someday you'll understand.

Someday. Her mother always said that.

Now she saw her grandparents only in the summer when she visited them for a month. Her grandfather never mentioned Serena's mother's name, his daughter's name, but he loved Serena. It was the same with her uncles. They would tease her at dinner about the tortillas she helped her grandmother make.

Is this what they call a tortilla in Los Angeles?

Uncle Aurelio was her favorite. He was the handsomest of the brothers, and he adored Serena. On his day off he would take her riding in his pick up truck, and when his friends asked about her blue eyes he would answer in Spanish too fast for Serena to understand. She had lost much of her Spanish since leaving there. Her mother never spoke it. Everyone in the family except her grandmother worked in the fields, long days, hot days, under the sun.

After her bath she put on clean pajamas and sat at her mother's vanity table. She turned on the lights that surrounded the mirrors and studied her face, her father's face. On the table there was a framed snapshot of him standing with her mother pregnant with Serena. He's wearing his sailor's uniform. In back of them you can see the big guns of his ship. His name was Hal. Hal Martin.

Our name is like your maiden name, Mama. Martinez.

Yes.

How did my father die?

There was an explosion on his ship. Someday I'll tell you the story. Someday.

Now, absorbed by her image, she made up her face, eyeliner, mascara, lipstick. When she finished she used the eyebrow pencil to put a beauty spot on her cheek. Her grandmother had a natural one. Serena could tell she was very vain about it. When the old lady was dressed for church taking one last look at herself in the hallway mirror she would turn it toward the mirror and touch it lightly with her fingertip.

While she was heating up some soup for her supper she heard a crash next door. It was followed by shouting. They were still fighting. She wondered if she would have to call the police. She hoped not. She'd have to give them her name, and when they came they might want to talk to her, come into the apartment even. Some instinct told her to avoid that. Under her mother's bed was a locked suitcase stored there for safekeeping as a favor to Howard, a friend of Ron's. Howard dressed in black leather and rode a motor cycle, and he looked like Johnny Depp. When Serena told him that, about Johnny Depp, he didn't say anything even though she could tell from his eyes that he liked hearing it. Watch a man's eyes, Serena heard her mother tell her friend Gloria one day when the two women were talking on the phone. They give themselves away with their eyes. Ever since she heard her mother say that Serena studied everyone's eyes, not just men's, and she guarded her own, careful not to let her thoughts show in them.

What's in the suitcase, Mama?

Some papers.

What kind of papers?

I don't know, some family business. Howard doesn't have a place of his own yet, and he doesn't want to store them in a locker. It's only for a week or two. Don't mention it to anyone, Serena. It's our secret.

Why doesn't he keep them at Ron's house?

Because Ron is never home, and he can get at them easier if they're here.

Do you use drugs, Mama?

No. Of course not.

Does Howard?

No. Why are you talking like this, about drugs?

Sister has been talking about them in school.

By the time she finished the soup things were quiet again next door. After she finished washing up she took off the makeup and settled again on the sofa to watch TV.

The telephone startled her awake. In the kitchen she turned on the light and looked at the clock on the stove. It was after midnight. She reached for the phone on the wall.

Is this Serena Martin?

Yes.

This is Detective Morris, Los Angeles Police Department.

Yes?

A couple of police officers are on the way over there to talk to you. I wanted to call you first, since it's so late, to give you some notice.

My mother isn't here.

I know that.

Is she all right?

The officers are on their way. They'll explain.

He hung up without saying goodbye.

Serena thought of the suitcase under her mother's bed. Maybe she could hide it, but where? There was only the bedroom closet and one in the bathroom where they kept the towels and sheets. This apartment. Not even a place to hide things. While she waited for the police the man next door went out, swearing loudly and slamming the door so hard that it shook the wall they shared. She hoped her mother was OK. She had a feeling that the police visit had something to do with the suitcase. Ever since Howard had left it there had been lots of phone calls with messages to have Howard call Ron or Ron call Howard.

Doesn't Ron have a phone either?

Yes, but he keeps it unlisted.

Why?

Because of his business, he doesn't want to be bothered at home. What kind of business?

Real estate.

The policeman was tall and handsome, and he

smelled like leather and clean wool. It filled the room just like her mothers body lotion did when she was there. A pair of handcuffs hanging from his belt clanked when he sat down, and he had to adjust the holster holding his gun in order to sit comfortably. He had brown hair that stuck to his head in damp curls when he took off his hat, and when he smiled his teeth shone white and even under his mustache. He told Serena he had a little girl five years old. He seemed nervous, but his voice was gentle, like his eyes. The woman with him was nice, too. She had on a blue suit with a white blouse open at the collar. She sat on the sofa and put her big black handbag on the floor beside her. Serena sat next to her. She told Serena that her name was Margaret, that she was a social worker, and that she had some very sad news. She reached for Serena's hand.

It's your mother. Something bad happened on the boat tonight. Some men came aboard while it was docked in the Marina, and there was a shooting. The man with your mother, Ron Bergeron, is dead, and your mother is seriously wounded. She's in County Hospital in critical condition. Serena stared at Margaret. No one said anything. Now she was sure that there was a connection between what happened on Ron's boat and the bag under her mother's bed. Concern for that bag and the trouble that probably went with it flooded over the fear for her mother's well being that had begun to grip Serena's heart when she first heard the news. She should have hidden that suitcase, but it was too late now.

Don't mention it to anyone, Serena. It's our secret.

The policeman shifted his position in the chair rattling the hand cuffs and sending out another whiff of his man smell.

Do you have any family in the city?

Up north, outside of Gilroy. My grandparents.

Do you have their telephone number?

Margaret went to the phone in the kitchen to make the call. Serena heard her ask if there was someone there who spoke English. Her grandmother must have answered the telephone. It was in the hallway outside her grandparents' bedroom. Her grandfather and her uncles slept very soundly. Only the rooster crowing at sunrise could awaken them easily.

Margaret called from the kitchen for the policeman to come to the phone. Serena heard him tell her grandmother in slow Spanish that there had been an accident. Her grandmother must have become hysterical, because there was a loud crying coming from the receiver, as the policeman whispered to Margaret. Serena went to the kitchen and took the receiver from the policeman. Putting it to her ear she listened to her grandmother wail. She waited for a pause in the crying.

Abuelita, esta Serena.

The old lady recognizing a familiar voice quieted down. Serena told her in Spanish, slower even than the policeman's, to wake up one of her sons.

Aurelio, levante Tio Aurelio.

She handed the phone to Margaret. When she finished on the phone Margaret asked Serena there was anyone who could come and stay with her until her relatives got there. She thought of her mother's friend, Gloria, the manicurist from the shop. She could tell Gloria about the suitcase if she had to. That is if the policeman and Margaret weren't there to search for it and maybe get her mother into even more trouble.

The policeman had to go pick up Gloria whose car was in the garage getting new brakes. Margaret followed him out the door and stood talking softly with him on the balcony. Serena's stomach felt like it did when she was in church waiting in line for her turn in the confessional where she would have to confess some intimate sin that had to do with her body. At such times she would shiver, and she found it hard to keep her hands still. Now it was worse, because there was no screen to protect her from being seen. Margaret would see and grow suspicious. Supposing they found the suitcase?

Don't mention to anyone, Serena. It's our secret. Margaret came back inside and closed the door. Serena offered to make tea.

That would be lovely.

While she was in the kitchen she heard Margaret call. Where do you go to school?

She ran the water harder and pretended not to hear. Margaret didn't pursue it. Alone in the kitchen Serena felt her composure coming back. All she had to do was to stay calm until they were gone. After that she could decide what to do next. When the tea was ready she put the cups, spoons, sugar, and a small pitcher of milk on a tray and brought it to the living room.

How nice.

While she was pouring the tea, she saw Margaret pick up and look at the book Serena had been reading.

Have you ever been to Hawaii, Serena?

Yes, my mother and I went there for our vacation. It was a lie. She'd have to confess.

Was it nice?

It was the best vacation we ever had. We stayed at the Royal Hawaiian, right on Waikiki Beach. It's an old hotel, but very luxurious. In the sunlight it's pink like cotton candy. From our room you could see Diamond Head. During the day we went to the beach in front of the hotel. Only the hotel guests can use it, and the bellhops bring your lunch to you right on the sand. It never gets too hot on the beach, because of the Trade Winds. They keep the temperature just right.

Did you swim?

Every day. The water is lukewarm. You don't get

any shock when you go in like you do at the beach here.

I've heard of that hotel. It's quite famous.

What I liked best about it was the garden. When you walk there at night in the moonlight the air smells of lotus blossoms.

I don't think I've ever smelled lotus blossoms.

They smell like pineapple.

Oh, how beautiful.

We ate steak practically every night. My mother said since we were on vacation we could be piggy, so we had hot fudge sundaes, too, after the steak.

I always have steak, too, when I go out.

One night we went to a nightclub that had a floorshow. There were hula dancers and Hawaiian drums, and at the finale a volcano on the stage spouted real flames. A cute boy with his parents at the next table asked me to dance. At first I said no thank you, but my mother said oh go ahead. He didn't dance very well. He was kind of stiff and nervous. I was, too. Pretty soon, though, we relaxed, and by the time the music stopped I was sorry it was over. His name was Jeff, and he was from Milwaukee.

I went to college in Milwaukee.

The flight home was over-booked, so they put us on a later one and upgraded us to first class. We had steak again.

It sounds wonderful. I hope I get to go there someday.

Serena excused herself and went to the bathroom. Sitting on the toilet she tried to think up another story to tell. Then she heard Gloria and the policeman come in. She might not need another one. When she came out of the bathroom Gloria and the policeman were sitting in the living room and Margaret was talking on the phone in the kitchen.

She's here with us and a friend of her mother's.

Gloria hugged Serena. Oh baby, baby. Her hair, bleached platinum blond, felt like straw against Serena's face.

Margaret held her hand. Try to think of your mother as she was when you were in Hawaii, when you were so happy together. I'll see you tomorrow when I come by to talk to your uncle. She gave her cell phone number to Gloria.

Serena stood by the door. The policeman touched her cheek as he went out. Margaret kissed her on the forehead. She locked the door behind them.

Gloria looked confused. What did she mean about Hawaii?

I told her my mother and I were saving for a trip. I said we were planning to go. She must have misunderstood.

NITRATE FILM

Mavis Chapman straightened the photograph of herself that hung on the wall in back of the counter of Sam's Hollywood Cleaners. The picture, taken in the early Forties when she was known as Louise Leonard, hung next to Myrna Loy's, whom Mavis was said to resemble. Mavis's photo used to hang on the wall near the door where no one ever looked, next to a shot of a funny looking kid named Skip Orkney. She switched it one day when Saverio the owner wasn't around. He never noticed. She brought in the headshot when she came there to work, almost ten years ago, after she retired from the cosmetics department of the May Company Wilshire, a job she had taken when the studio started giving the small parts that were hers to younger more eager actresses. Soon after retiring from the May Company she found that Social Security and a small union pension couldn't be stretched far enough. One night in Musso's bar she met Saverio who owned four dry cleaning stores. During a brief affair, he had a wife, five kids and a lot of grandchildren, he offered her a job in the Hollywood store near her apartment. It was his way of saying thanks for sleeping with him, and after she'd been working there for a week it was obvious that he'd lost interest in her sexually. Like everyone else in Hollywood Saverio craved variety.

Mavis could tell he was on the make when he would tear up the ticket and wave away the charge on a woman's order. The women ran the gamut from old but well preserved, like Mavis, to young starlet types who didn't mind putting out if the bill was big enough. Today, she was out of sorts. She'd had a Pap smear earlier in the week, part of her annual physical, and today was call in day. Angel, one of the pressers, hadn't helped matters when he announced that morning that his sister had been diagnosed with cancer and given no more than six months.

"Jew jis neber know," he kept saying through the hissing steam, "jew jis neber know." He must have said it a fifty times since he first told them the news.

"I hear that, honey," said Lavinia, the other presser. She had answered him every time.

Mavis was ready to scream. When Saverio stopped by and had a temper tantrum over some slipcovers that had shrunk in the cleaning process she was grateful for the diversion.

At four-thirty she called the doctor's office and was told that the test was negative. The thought of a martini at Musso's carried her through until closing time. After she locked the door behind Angel and Lavinia she took the cash from the register and went to the back of the store where she counted it and dropped it through a slot in the floor safe behind the hot water tank. Then she changed from the gym shoes she wore when she worked into a pair of medium-heel pumps she'd recently bought. Shoes were her weakness, and she always bought the best. They served to call attention to the only good features she had left, her legs and ankles. Everything else, sagging and worn out, needed propping up or outright camouflage. She put the gym shoes on the shelf near Angel's presser under a picture of Our Lady of Guadalupe. She often left them there, but today it looked disrespectful, so she moved them to Lavinia's shelf beneath an autographed shot of Gladys Knight and the Pips.

At Musso's she parked her car in the lot at the back and walked around to the Hollywood Boulevard entrance. She never used the back door off the lot. She liked to make an entrance even if no one noticed. Larry was on tonight behind the bar. As soon as he spotted her he went to the register and picked up an envelope, placing it in front of her as she sat down.

"You won the pool, eleven correct picks , two hundred and forty bucks."

"I can't believe it. I don't know a thing about football. I just picked the teams from the cities I've been in."

"You've been in the right cities, kid. How do you want it tonight, up or on the rocks?"

"If you're talking about a martini I'll have it up. I'm celebrating."

Larry gave her a thumbs up and reached for the silver shaker. Mavis watched while he showed off making the drink, pouring the gin from an exaggerated height above the shaker and moving the top of the bottle in close as he tapered off the flow. God, she thought, don't we love to be watched.

"I got a call back on the Honda commercial," said Larry.

"I'll keep my fingers crossed."

"I could use a break." He put a chilled glass in front of her and poured. "You want two olives?"

"Why not?"

"Anyone ever told you you've got sexy hands?" He stage whispered it.

"No, you bullshit artist, they never have."

Before he could respond another customer came in, and he moved his charm down the bar, away from her, as if it were on ball bearings. The customer, a man in a business suit, asked what kind of beer they had, and Larry, holding the man's eyes with his own, reeled off the brands. Mavis felt a pang of jealousy as she swallowed her first sip of the icy gin. Besides the man and herself there were two guys at the bar speaking a language she didn't recognize.

She wondered if Joel would be in tonight. She hadn't seen him for a week. She hoped he was all right. She suspected that Joel, who worked in the film archive of a studio in Burbank, didn't take care of himself very well. Mavis had always done that, taken care of herself. She went for a long walk two or three times a week, and she ate right, indulging herself only enough to keep life interesting. Years ago when she was working in the business a guy she was seeing, also an actor, told her that their bodies were the only capital they could count on. He said it while he stared at his naked reflection in the mirror rigged on the ceiling over his bed. Mavis took another sip of gin and wondered if he was still alive.

"Hi Mavis."

"Joel, I was just thinking of you."

"I'm glad someone was."

Larry came over and put a paper napkin on the bar. "What'll it be, Sport?"

"I think I'll have a Compari and soda, Lare."

"You've got it."

"Put it on my tab," said Mavis.

"You don't have to do that," said Joel.

"I know I don't. I want to."

Larry poured the drink and went back to the other end of the bar where he resumed chopping limes.

"God," said Joel, "he's gorgeous."

"So are you."

"No I'm not. I know I'm attractive, but gorgeous is something else."

"This town is full of gorgeous," said Mavis.

"Do you think he's gay?"

"How should I know? Why don't you ask him?"

"I have, in a thousand little ways."

"And?"

"I'm still not sure, but I suspect no."

"Why don't you just come right out with it?"

"For reasons I find hard to explain. Anyway he isn't attracted to me."

"So? There's more than one pebble on the beach,as my mother used to say."

"My mother says that too," said Joel.

"Everybody's mother says that. How's your job going?"

"Good. I haven't forgotten about your film, but my boss has been away, and I've got lots of stuff on my plate right now."

"I wasn't pushing," said Mavis.

"Things are crazy at the studio. We're involved in a big TV buy. No one can think of anything else."

"Hey, I understand. It's a crazy business."

The restaurant was filling up rapidly, and by the time she had finished her martini the bar had gotten crowded. Joel was talking to a guy his age who kept saying he couldn't believe he was finally in Hollywood. She paid her bill and got up to leave.

"Thanks for the drink, Mavis," said Joel. "My turn next time."

"You'd better not forget."

Joel laughed and went back to his conversation. Mavis wondered if he would leave with the guy.

On her way home she stopped at a drug store to pick up some hair color. Standing in front of the display she thought about going lighter. She considered champagne. It looked good on the model decorating the box who must have been all of nineteen, but Mavis was afraid it would look too white on her, and she decided to stay with ash blond. The woman ahead of her in the check out was buying a lot of stuff. While she waited Mavis studied the rack of condoms near the register. They came in colors now and some were marked extra-large.

She thought again about Joel. She hoped he didn't think she was being a pest about the film, but it had been on her mind ever since the night in the bar when he mentioned a program at the studio archive to collect and preserve the screen tests of as many stars as they could get their hands on. Mavis had thought immediately of her own screen test, and her heart leapt. It was done in the Thirties when the hunt was on for Scarlet O'Hara. They dressed her in a hoop skirt that swayed below a bodice cut to emphasize her breasts,painfully pushed up with wads of toilet paper. Her hair was curled in the ante-bellum style. Except for the dreams that rode on it there was nothing to distinguish it from thousands of others done at the time.

"I have the film of my screen test," she told Joel that night.

"Oh?"

"Do you think they might want it?"

"I don't know," said Joel. "I think they're going

after the more established stars, no offense intended, but I could check."

"I'd be happy to let them have it."

"I'll let you know."

I'll let you know. Mavis wished she had a nickel for every time she heard that line. Her third, and last, husband had said it when he boarded the Twentieth Century Limited for New York. He was talking about when she could put their things in storage and follow him. She never saw him again. He went right on through New York to London where he fell in with a bad crowd, worse than the one he ran with out here, and drank himself to death. I'll let you know. After they said that you were supposed to go on about your business like you weren't even thinking about how you were going to pay the rent if they didn't let you know. Her agent, Morrie Weingarten, a mean son of a bitch if ever there was one, used to say, "A hungry actor gives off a smell that makes even a receptionist want to head for the hills. If you want it so bad your teeth ache, don't let it show." Mavis unlocked the door to her apartment. The screen test, inside a film can, sat on the coffee table, ready to go.

"Don't look at me like that," she said to it. "I'll let you know."

The next morning, Joel Seligman opened his eyes directly into Brad Pitt's, staring down at him from the poster on the wall opposite the bed. On automatic, he did all the morning things. When he was dressed for work he read his mail while he revved up his brain with coffee and a jolt of sugar from a day old jelly doughnut. There was a card from his dentist to remind him it was check up time. A notice from the insurance company informed him that his car insurance premium was going up. He'd been expecting that after a fender bender in the parking lot of an after hours club in North Hollywood. There was a letter from his mother saying everything was fine on their end along with a p.s., she always put it in the p.s., telling him to be careful and to take care of himself. As always it annoyed him, not because he didn't appreciate the love in back of it, but because she still saw him as a child. The telephone rang. It was his ex-girlfriend Deborah. She wanted to meet him for a drink after work. He made a date to meet her at Musso's.

When he arrived at work there was a note on his desk from his boss, Wes Van Holt, saying he wanted to take a meeting first thing. Joel was pretty sure Wes was alcoholic, and he disliked meeting with him first thing in the morning when Wes's hands trembled moving the Styrofoam cup from his desk to his mouth. Furthermore his face would be liverish at that hour and he tended to be irascible. Joel could usually avoid him by spending the morning in the film vault where he worked alone. After lunch, Wes, color restored and steady of hand again, acted normal, or as Joel told his friend Louie who worked in the studio property department, as normal as anyone gets in this town.

"Have you ever heard of Benjamin Goodliffe?" asked Wes, as Joel helped himself to coffee.

"No."

"What the hell do you mean, no?"

"Is he an actor?"

"No, he's the bouncer at the Hard Rock Café."

"OK, you win."

"His screen test showed up," said Wes.

"What's he done?"

"He's dead."

"What did he do?"

"That's what I want you to find out. Get his filmography and check if we've got any of his stuff."

Joel took a sip of coffee while he decided whether or not it was a good time to bring up Mavis's screen test. He went for it. "Do you have any specific guidelines for accepting or rejecting something for the screen test collection?"

Wes wiped some spilled coffee off the top of his desk with a tissue. "Not yet, and please don't bug me. You start setting guidelines and you become responsible. You get too responsible and sure as shit you end up with your ass in the unemployment line."

"Do you want to see any of Goodliffe's films if we have them?"

"Write me a memo," said Wes. "I'll get back to you."

Joel found one of Goodliffe's pictures in the

vault, something called, "Come To Xanadu." Goodliffe was billed fifth. He called around town looking for the other stuff. Of the twenty-two pictures credited to Goodliffe, he was able to locate four. Just as he was finishing the memo to Wes one of the archivists to whom he had spoken called back to say that the print he had was no good. It had never been transferred to safety film, and the nitrate on which it had been printed had disintegrated.

"All that remains of Benjamin Goodliffe is a can full of brown powder," said the archivist.

Joel re-wrote the memo. He thought of Mavis's screen test. Chances are it too had rotted away. On his way to lunch he stopped in the men's room where he ran into Wes. Shunning the urinal next to the one Wes was using, Joel opted for a stall. "I've located three of Goodliffe's pictures," he said over his shoulder.

"Who?"

"Goodliffe, the bouncer at the Hard Rock."

"What the hell are you talking about?

"I'm writing you a memo. Enjoy your lunch."

He was gone when Joel stepped out of the stall. Wes was an avid luncher, keeping a Rolodex with the names and phone numbers of the people he ate with. The file was color coded with Wes's equals getting a white card and superiors accorded pink, blue, yellow, on up to peach, a color reserved for vice-presidents and such. There was room on the cards for notations, heavily abbreviated, as to the restaurant, who paid, and what and how much the person drank. One lunch hour when Joel was sneaking a look at the file Wes returned unexpectedly. Joel made the excuse that he was looking for the number of a film lab. Wes, not fooled, suggested that in the future Joel use the phone book or call information. Making his way across the crowded studio lot Joel concentrated on not bumping into anyone. Louie was waiting for him in front of the cafeteria. "I just saw Eddie Fisher," he said.

"What was he doing?"

"Getting into a limo."

"How did he look?"

"Pretty good, considering."

"Considering what?"

"That he's had enough surgery to make two child stars out of what they removed."

"That's a shitty thing to say. We're all going to be old someday."

"We hope," said Louie.

They sat at a table outside on the patio.

"Deborah called this morning," said Joel.

"What did she want? As if I didn't know."

"She wants to have a drink after work."

"You haven't asked what I think," said Louie, "but I think you should think about this very carefully."

"You're right. And I have."

"I'll mind my own business. Do you ever think about having sex with her?"

"Not anymore."

"I'm not sure I could get it up for a woman."

"I can get it up for anything that moves," said Joel.

"So you're always telling me."

After lunch he returned Deborah's call and arranged to meet her at Musso's after work. They had known each other since their first year in college when they were in the same dorm. Autumn was late that year, and students were still lying out on the grass in October studying in their bathing suits. Joel had a weakness for blondes with suntans, and he noticed her right away. The fact that she was always alone interested him further. He took to spreading his blanket near hers. Lying on his stomach and protected by his sunglasses he watched her over the top of his book. After they'd gotten to know each other she told him she could tell that he'd been looking at her because he never turned a page.

"I could have been studying something complex."

"You were," she said.

It was that self-assurance that turned him on and pushed him over the line into love. He'd been there a few times before, but not like that. When he was thirteen he was in love, although he didn't call it that, with his patrol leader in Scouts, a kid two years older. Joel started dressing like the other boy, and he wanted to be with him all the time. Once they went camping together, just the two of them, and Joel was breathless with the possibilities in being alone with him in a tent in the middle of the woods. But nothing happened. Except for smoking the cigarettes his hero had stolen from home they did nothing the authors of the Boy Scout Manual wouldn't have approved of. Joel's girlfriend in high school was a cheerleader. They went steady for two years, and in the yearbook poll they were voted cutest couple. Virgins, they had sex for the first time the day of the senior picnic. That exchange, which also took place in the woods, made him eager to get away to college where sexuality, like a big glittering city, lay waiting to be explored. He and Deborah started sleeping together soon after they met. Her roommate made things easy by going home every weekend. She had more experience than he did, and the self-assurance that turned him on she brought to their bed. In their second year, over coffee the first night back after a summer in which they'd been apart, she told him she'd had an affair with another woman, the swimming instructor at the camp where she'd worked.

"Where does that leave us?" he asked.

"I'm not sure, but let's cool it for a while."

They never had sex again, but they stayed close friends all through college and up to the present. Actually, Joel had been relieved. He'd spent the summer as a fire watcher, living alone on a raised platform in the Oregon wilderness where the trees and the solitude had triggered fantasies of the camping trip with the patrol leader. By the end of the summer those fantasies had overtaken in frequency the ones of him and Deborah in her narrow dormitory bed. By the time they graduated from college and moved to Los Angeles she was in a committed relationship, and he had explored a larger area of the glittering city than he anticipated when he was a freshman.

She hadn't arrived yet when he got to Musso's after work. Larry, with a new short haircut, was behind the bar.

"You got a call from a lady named Deborah. She said she'd be a little late. That was a half hour ago."

"Thanks, Lare. Hey, I like the new haircut."

"Thanks. I do, too. My agent says I'll be able to go up for more straight businessman stuff."

"As opposed to the gay businessman stuff?"

"What are you drinking, Sport?"

"I'll have a pint of Guinness."

Deborah came in and stood in the doorway looking around. Joel watched her find him and make her way towards him. God, he thought, we could have a good looking kid. He got off the bar stool to hug her. Larry was waiting with a smile when she sat down. "What can I get for you?" His eyes went after hers, but hers darted.

She turned to Joel. "What are you having?"

"He's having Guinness," said Larry.

"I'll have the same." She said it to Joel.

"And a Stout it is," said Larry.

"We sold a script," said Deborah. She and her partner, Melissa, wrote free-lance for TV.

"Holy shit, that's fantastic."

"We have to have it in by the end of the month. Then Melissa goes to Hawaii for two weeks. It's her parents' thirty fifth, and Karl's taking the whole family."

"Aren't you invited?"

"Hardly. Karl can't deal with it."

She and Melissa, whose father was Karl the Hardware King, owned a house in Laurel Canyon. They had been trying unsuccessfully for a year to adopt a child. It was Melissa's idea that one of them have a baby. They decided upon artificial insemination, and, given Deborah's past relationship with Joel, he seemed to be the logical choice to be the sperm donor. Deborah, being the younger of the two, agreed to bear the child.

She brought it up a month ago at a friend's wedding after they'd drunk a lot of champagne and were dancing close. She assured Joel that all the financial arrangements would be ironclad. The child would know Joel as its father, and he would be allowed, encouraged even, to participate in its upbringing. Deborah was convinced that they were all sufficiently enlightened to bring it all off in a civilized manner.

Joel was intrigued. The fact that he wasn't the

marrying kind hadn't freed him from an atavistic urge to make a biological mark. High on wedding wine and holding her close while they danced he told her that he liked the sound of it, that he would love to have a child of theirs. He asked her to give him some time to live with it before he gave her a definite answer. He was pretty sure she was going to ask for that tonight, and he was ready to say yes. It was an unconventional way to go, and he had been reared to accept conventionality as good for the order of things. In the end, however, he decided it wasn't a word he wanted written on his tombstone.

Now, ignoring the drink in front of her, Deborah put forth a plan. While Melissa was in Hawaii, she and Joel could use the opportunity to conceive the child. Arrangements had been made for several appointments with a fertility clinic. She spoke in that confident manner that always turned him on, and the urge to yield to her washed over him like a warm wave. He thought of his sperm inside of her, and he felt himself getting hard. He wondered if she had thought about conceiving in the more traditional way. He told her he was ready to go forward. "My mother and father are going to be very happy."

"I wish I could say that about mine and Melissa's," she said.

"People have a way of changing when they see their grandchildren, and you know this one can't miss in the looks department."

"I know," she said. I thought of that. I'll call you over the weekend. I have to go. We're having people for dinner."

"What's the name of the show you're writing for?"

"They keep changing it." She got off the barstool. "It's about a successful woman attorney in D.C. who adopts a set of identical Korean twins."

"Korean?"

"Don't ask. If it goes there's a chance we'll get on staff."

"What studio?"

"Paramount."

He stood and took her into his arms. "Tell Melissa I said hi."

"Yes." She stayed in his arms while he buried his face in her hair. She took a deep breath. "Oh, Joel," she sighed, "I'm so happy." Then she kissed him on the cheek and hurried away.

"Ready for another one, Sport?"

"Thanks, Lare."

Mavis Chapman had come in and sat down while Joel was talking with Deborah. He moved over to sit beside her. "Hey Louise Leonard, they want your screen test for the archive."

"Really?" said Mavis. "They want it? Well I'll be goddamned."

"Tell me something," said Joel. "Did you ever have it transferred to safety film?"

"I don't even know that that means," said Mavis.

The next morning at Sam's Hollywood Cleaners Mavis searched the shelf near Angel's presser for the bottle of aspirin that he kept there. Neither he nor Lavinia were in yet. She was early. She'd had too much to drink last night and her sleep was fitful. This morning a hangover waited in the wings ready to take center stage if she didn't get control of it with aspirin and two or three glasses of water. The water would have her in and out of the john all morning, but what the hell, she thought as she sat down on the cold toilet seat in the small lavatory at the back of the shop, I never claimed to be perfect. The sense of relief, peace really, that came over her when Joel told her they wanted her screen test was something she hadn't felt in a long time. It was just like in the old days when, after a long hiatus between jobs, her contract up for renewal, Morrie's office would call and say the studio had scheduled her for another picture, and the contract looked good for another year. She would go out and celebrate then too, her burden lightened, the rent paid for the foreseeable future. Louise Leonard had made it to a film archive. Jesus Christ. She wished her mother were alive, so she could know it too.

"You look like you got laid last night," said Lavinia.

Saverio came by at noon, on his way to the bank. He asked her to have lunch with him, something he hadn't done in years. They went to Yamashiro's up in the hills above Sunset. He was talkative and gallant the way he was when she was sleeping with him. She wondered if he had a new girlfriend. On her way home she stopped and bought a pair of shoes she had been admiring. Then she got a turkey sandwich at a deli and rented the only film of hers that had made it to DVD. When she got home she had a bath, and in her robe ate the sandwich and watched the film. She played a singer in a road house on the outskirts of an unnamed city. In its day it was known as a B picture, but now they called it film noir.

Later that week Joel Seligman entered Louise Leonard's name and bio into the computer. He typed a memo to Wes Van Holt informing him of the addition to the archive. He then reversed two letters in Wes's email address and sent the memo. He looked at the film can containing Mavis's screen test and considered opening it, but he decided not to. Instead, he picked it up and carried it to the vault where he placed it in the L section between Lotte Lenya and Joan Leslie.

Richard Frattali is a founding member of The Groundlings, LA's premier improvisational comedy troupe now in its thirty-fifth year. His work was honored as "Best of the 70's" in the troupe's 30th Anniversary Gala at the Henry Fonda Theater in Hollywood. His writing for television includes the popular sitcom, Gimme A Break. He has written several educational films on the subject of teenagers and drugs. He served in the U.S. Navy as a gunnery officer on the USS Canberra, a guided missile cruiser. He has taught public speaking and communications skills at the United States Naval Academy at Annapolis. He is a member of the Screen Actors Guild and the Writers Guild of America. He lives in Northern California.